W9-DFN-064

Landmark BOOKS

05/24
STAND PRICE
$ 3.00

STONEWALL
JACKSON

STONEWALL JACKSON

JONATHAN DANIELS

Illustrated by William Moyers

RANDOM HOUSE · NEW YORK

FIRST PRINTING

© Copyright, 1959, by Jonathan Daniels
All rights reserved under International and Pan-American
Copyright Conventions. Published in New York by Random
House, Inc., and simultaneously in Toronto, Canada,
by Random House of Canada, Limited.
Library of Congress Catalog Card Number: 59–5519
Manufactured in the United States of America
by H. Wolff, New York

CONTENTS

STONEWALL
JACKSON

✵ 1 ✵

Small Boy and Big Fish

In the 1830s in that high back part of Virginia which is now West Virginia, a man had to stand on his two strong legs. Also, he needed to understand that his word, once given, must be as good as his bond. Such qualities were shown by Cummins Jackson's barrels and the big fish of his young orphan nephew, Tom Jackson.

Uncle Cummins was a hearty frontier gentleman.

That was something very different from the gentlemen of the older Virginia which ran down from the mountains to the proud, starched and high-collared tidewater. A man so tall that he had to stoop when he came through doors, Cummins Jackson had lands and properties, horses and dogs, a few slaves—and big muscles. Once he won a bet by hoisting a barrel of hard cider over his head and drinking from the bunghole. Sometimes he came out of his mill carrying a barrel of flour under each arm.

Tom was not noted for such feats. A recurrent stomach ache troubled him even as a child. He was a reed-slim, quiet, wistful boy. He worked well. Sometimes he shared the fun. Though he never rode like a graceful horseman, he followed happily when Uncle Cummins, with the dogs baying ahead, chased the fox and hurried to the treeing of the coons. Sometimes even as a wiry boy he rode as jockey on Uncle Cummins' horses in the high-stake races which were as characteristic of the frontier country as its hard, plain religion.

Tom occasionally played the fiddle but the general feeling was that there were better fiddlers in the upper

Monongahela country. There is no record that he danced while others played the homemade fiddles and buckskin banjos. Always dutiful, generally solemn, he sometimes seemed almost painfully honest. Certainly he seemed so one day when, as a boy of eleven, he came down the road from the heavily shaded banks of the West Fork of the Monongahela River. He was carrying a three-foot pike over his shoulder. There seemed to be almost more fish than boy.

He was on a business errand. Conrad Kester, the local gunsmith, had made a bargain to buy from him at a fixed price all the fish of a certain size he caught. This one met all the specifications. On his way to deliver it Tom passed the house of well-to-do Colonel John Talbott. The Colonel called from his porch.

"That's a nice fish you got there, Tom. What'll you take for it?"

"This fish is sold, Colonel Talbott."

"But I'll give you a dollar for it."

"I can't take it, sir. This fish is sold to Mr. Kester."

"Now, Tom," the Colonel argued, "I'll give you a dollar and a quarter. Surely he won't give you more than that."

Tom was polite but stubborn.

"Colonel Talbott, I have an agreement with Mr. Kester to furnish him fish of a certain length for fifty cents each. He has taken some too short. Now he is going to get this big one for fifty cents."

The gunsmith got it. Also, so the story goes, he offered to raise his own price to a dollar for the prize pike. Tom declined. A bargain was a bargain. His word was his bond. Some thought then that Tom was a little stiff in his notion of his responsibility. Some thought that later, too. Such exaggerated notions of obligation helped build the opinion that he carried his ideas about duty to exaggerated extremes. As a boy then, his character was all he had.

Tom or Thomas Jonathan Jackson—nobody then dreamed that his enduring name would become Stonewall—was born at Clarksburg on January 21, 1824. He was the third child of Jonathan Jackson, a young lawyer with high hopes but few resources, and Julia Neale Jackson, a pretty, delicate young woman. Then two years later came one of those epidemics of typhoid fever which hit big and little places like the plague. Tom's seven-year-old sister Elizabeth contracted it. So did their father who nursed her. Both died, the father on the day before another child was born.

Julia and her babies were penniless. The Masonic Fraternity of which Jonathan had been a member gave them a one-room house to live in. Townspeople provided little jobs for Julia. She struggled four years, then was married again, not bettering herself, to a good man but poor provider, Captain Blake Woodson. Others had to take care of the children. Tom came home from the house of his Uncle Cummins to his mother's deathbed when he was seven years old. He never forgot that homecoming. And two years later even his stepfather was dead. Sickness, insecurity and death surrounded his childhood. Perhaps then and later it was not strange that some of his defenses seemed to others almost eccentricities.

There was nothing odd about his activities. He was fishing for profit when he was eleven. At thirteen he went off with his brother Warren on an adventurous business along the shores of the Ohio and Mississippi rivers. They cut and sold logs to the wonderful new wood-burning steamboats. They came back with malaria instead of a fortune. And at Uncle Cummins' lively establishment again, Tom managed crews of slaves cutting timber in the great woods for his uncle's sawmill. Uncle Cummins got him a job as an "engineering assistant" in the construction of a turnpike from Parkersburg to Staunton. Then at seventeen, though some people thought he was too young for the position, Tom was made constable of the Freeman Creek District of Lewis County.

That did not mean that Tom was a romantic law officer on the frontier rounding up desperadoes. His business was not catching bad men but serving legal papers and collecting little debts. Some of those who owed money were not easy characters to handle. It took tactics and strategy to deal with them. One such man had long dodged paying money he owed a widow. Tom decided to seize and hold his horse for the debt. It was a stern rule of the frontier, however, that no man's horse could be taken while he was riding it. Tom waited until the owner dismounted at a livery stable, then quickly grabbed the reins. The fellow jumped back on the horse, regaining possession, and began slashing Tom with his whip. Young Jackson held on. He led the horse and rider toward the low-beamed stable door where the rider had to get off or be knocked off. Tom had clear possession then. The man had to pay what he owed or lose his horse. The widow got her money.

In those years Tom discovered that other people, sometimes when least expected, could use clever tactics, too. As a fisherman, woodcutter, road builder and constable, Tom was constantly studying hard to get ahead. One story is that he made a bargain with one of Uncle Cummins' slaves to furnish him pine knots by the light of which he studied long after dark. In return, Tom agreed to teach the slave to read and write. Each carried out his bargain. Young Jackson undoubtedly learned by the blaze. But as soon as the Negro was able to write his name, he signed it to a pass and slipped off by the Underground Railroad to Canada and freedom.

Tom was too modest about his own education. Schooling was generally inadequate in the back country of Virginia when he was a boy. Even in the older country toward tidewater, schools—or academies as they were called—were limited in number and available to few students, mostly the sons of the well-to-do.

Poor people got little schooling or none at all. However, hale and hearty Uncle Cummins, while no scholar himself, helped establish a little school in nearby Weston where Tom walked to his first classes. He was not a brilliant pupil. One of his teachers said later that "he learned slowly, but what he got in his head he never forgot."

Tom wanted to learn. He read not only by lightwood fire but in the shade of the trees. The two best-remembered books in his reading were the *Bible,* of course, and one other not much less important in his career. From a friend he secured a copy of *The Life of Francis Marion* by Parson Mason Weems. The parson made all his heroes super-good. Weems was responsible for the legend about young George Washington and the cherry tree. Tom read and reread his story of General Marion, the "Swamp Fox," whose swift, hard Revolutionary forays seem now almost to anticipate "Stonewall" Jackson's campaigns in the Valley of Virginia.

Tom taught school himself. In view of the poor schools and short terms provided then, that does not prove his learning. He taught two terms to the appar-

The fellow began slashing Tom with his whip

ent satisfaction of pupils and parents, however. He was less satisfied himself. Apparently the teaching made him realize how much more he had to learn. In seeking an opportunity for more education, he discovered the hard way how much he lacked. His Congressman had an appointment to make to the United States Military Academy established forty years before on the Hudson River at West Point, New York. There a boy could secure a free college education and a lifetime position as an officer in the United States Army. Three other boys also wanted the appointment, so the Congressman ordered a competitive examination. Tom took it. But another young fellow, an orphan, too, won the test. The door seemed closed on young Jackson's hope to be a soldier.

2

"What You Resolve to Be"

Some of Tom Jackson's friends murmured about his failure to get the appointment to West Point. They said he lost because the winner was the sweetheart of the daughter of the man who gave the examination. But Tom knew he had failed not because of a girl but because of math.

He settled down to study for whatever other opportunities might come. Then suddenly the winner of the exam came home. West Point, he said, was no place for him. He did not care for its grim discipline. Also, maybe he missed his girl. At any rate Tom sought a second chance. Many wanted to help the determined young man but one of his older friends asked him a bold question: Did he think his educational background was good enough for him to make the grade at the United States Military Academy? Tom did not brag.

"I am very ignorant," he said, "but I can make it up in study. I know I have the energy and I think I have the intellect."

With letters of recommendation, he hurried to Washington. From Clarksburg to Cumberland, Maryland, to the national capital, he went on horseback and by stage. Then he traveled on the first train he had ever seen. It was on the Baltimore and Ohio Railroad which reached Cumberland that year. His trip took him to Harpers Ferry at the meeting place of the Potomac and Shenandoah rivers above the valley he was to mark so much with his name and his nickname. In Washington his determination was impressive, too. On June 12, 1842, he received his appointment from

President Tyler's short-tempered Secretary of War, John C. Spencer. Spencer looked over young Jackson's endorsements.

"Young man, you have a good name. If anybody at West Point insults you, give 'em a good beating and charge it to me."

Tom was not expecting insults or planning quarrels. He was eager for opportunity. That was his first visit to any city and Washington then was only a town of 15,000 people. Charles Dickens, the English novelist, that year described it as a place of "spacious avenues that begin in nothing and lead nowhere." Tom did not linger to see its sights or lack of them, though he did take time to climb to the top of the then unfinished Capitol. Visible from it across the Potomac was Virginia. The plains of Manassas could be seen as well as the great house of Arlington, home of Robert Edward Lee, then a thirty-five-year-old captain in the United States Army.

Jackson hastened to West Point. Taking another man's place, he, of course, got there late. That brought him special attention from cadets who had already begun their work in the gray buildings above the river.

He attracted even more attention because of his bump-
kin appearance. West Point had special ideas of fitness.
Three years before Jackson arrived there were de-
mands in Congress that the academy be abolished because it was "a breeding ground of snobbery." Northerners and Westerners thought that it depended too
much for its social character and ideas upon the aris-
tocratic South. That was not the kind of South from
which Tom Jackson came.

He carried all his possessions in a pair of battered
saddlebags. His lank figure in homespun clothes was
crowned by a big, flopping, coarse felt hat. Apparently
it was the sort which country constables in the South
wore then and later. He stood awkward and gan-
gling above his big feet. When he took off his hat he
disclosed a great mop of brown hair. His blue eyes
were steady, however, and his lips firm.

He seemed funny to some of his classmates who
watched his arrival. Some Virginians were in the group.
Three of them, George Edward Pickett, Ambrose
Powell Hill and Dabney Herndon Maury were to become Confederate generals. They qualified as repre-
sentatives of the patrician South. All of them were

graduates of the academies to which young Virginia gentlemen were sent in those days by well-to-do parents anxious for correct education. Indeed, Maury had already graduated from the University of Virginia before he went to West Point. As an older cadet, Maury was perhaps a more understanding one. Some cadets laughed at the country newcomer. Maury only smiled a little and shook his hand.

"That fellow," he said, "looks as if he had come to stay."

Jackson stayed. He studied long after taps by the light of his barracks-room fire. He wrote maxims for himself in a little book he kept. Some were:

"Sacrifice your life rather than your word.

"Through life let your principal object be the discharge of duty.

"Resolve to perform what you ought; perform without fail what you resolve.

"Speak but what may benefit others or yourself; avoid trifling conversation."

Perhaps most important of all was his determined faith: "You may be whatever you resolve to be."

The young man of such mottoes was no gay blade

of the Point. He was not very social. Maury, who became his friend, felt that at first the gawky newcomer rebuffed his kindly attentions. Tom became acquainted at the academy, however, with men whom he was to know as friends and foes later. George Brinton McClellan, already something of the supposed "little Napoleon" whom Jackson was to confront on the Virginia Peninsula, was in his class. So were others he was to fight with and beside. In another class while Jackson was there was a cadet named Ulysses S. Grant, who was at least as rural in appearance when he arrived as Jackson when he came. Grant was not as duty-bound as Jackson. The cadets thought it was a joke when Grant was made a sergeant; they said he was made a non-commissioned officer because he could not keep step in the ranks. And in the class ahead of Jackson was Barnard E. Bee, a courtly cadet from South Carolina. Tom was to see more of him on fighting fields.

The boy from the Virginia back country got along very well with his classmates. Behind his gruff exterior his fellow cadets found a gentle sense of humor and unexpected kindness. He was not to be pushed around, however. One cadet who swapped his dirty rifle for

He seemed funny to some of his classmates

Jackson's gleaming one never tried it again. Generally, however, he seemed withdrawn because he was at work. Tom learned hard. Sometimes at the blackboard he so sweated at his task that the back of his jacket became wet with perspiration. He began slowly and from far behind, but his record steadily improved, month by month, year by year.

At his graduation in June, 1846, the sloppy black hat he had worn on his arrival was replaced by a majestic full-dress pompom hat. His gray coatee was brushed to flecklessness. His white cross-belts, brass buttons, black boots, all shone. Bands played such West Point airs as "On to Victory," and "The Dashing Sergeant White." A happy crowd of visitors, parents and girls looked on. Tom Jackson ("the General" other cadets called him in mocking honor of General Andrew Jackson) was still much alone in such a crowd.

Yet he had risen from the fifty-first place in his class during his first year to seventeenth at graduation. A story often repeated at West Point said that if he had a year more he would have been the class's number one man. In the process he had moved past some of those who had laughed at his countrified appearance when he first arrived. Maury, having already graduated from college before he came to the Point, had little difficulty with his studies. But as Virgina gentlemen taught in that State's best academies, Pickett and Hill did not do so well. Pickett, who was soon to be the first man over the parapets at Chapultepec and later led the charge which keeps his name at Gettysburg, barely got by as the bottom man in the class. Ambrose Hill, who was to ride with Jackson and to lead an army corps for Lee, was less fortunate. Deficient in math, he had to wait another year for his diploma.

More than customary excitement attended the graduation. The class of 1846 was to leave the academy directly for fighting in a foreign land. Six weeks before, Congress had declared war on Mexico. The country was excited, though some Northerners feared the war would extend the slavery they despised. Brevet Lieutenant T. J. Jackson found civilians marching—and not marching too well—when he went back to his native country on brief furlough. He saw old friends. Uncle Cummins looked older—as if he could probably pick up only one barrel at a time now. In his uniform Tom was less shy with "female acquaintances." But he did not linger long. Soon he moved with horses and guns in the Artillery which he, like Napoleon, had chosen as his arm of the service. Delays made him fear that he might miss the fighting. The war might be over before he had a chance at fame.

"I want to be in one battle," he said, not seeing much chance of it. He was to have his share before he was through.

3

Path to Glory

As eager to show himself as soldier as he had been to prove himself as student, Lieutenant Tom Jackson's fears that he might miss fighting in the Mexican War seemed at first justified. It was almost a year after his graduation before he saw any action. He had been sent first to the Texas-Mexican border country at a time when that front was quiet. But soon after he was in the midst of dramatic action as

a part of the great armada General Winfield Scott
gathered before the port of Vera Cruz. His soldiers
called Scott "Old Fuss and Feathers" because he was
a strict disciplinarian. His orders were welcome to
Jackson when Scott sent him in one of the waves of
boats toward the white and green beaches. Little resistance met the Americans on the shore, but in the
siege of the town Jackson worked with the advanced
batteries. A cannon ball narrowly missed him. He
sent plenty in return. In his first fighting his "gallant
and meritorious conduct" brought him a promotion.

He found that he enjoyed battle. He was cool under
fire. All his faculties were clearer then. He wanted, as
he always urged others, to "Press on." As an impatient
lieutenant, just turned twenty-three, he was even pri-
vately critical of General Scott, who had become a national hero in the War of 1812, when the siege of Vera
Cruz ended. Scott allowed the Mexicans to retire without hot, punishing pursuit. Such chivalry in the business
of war seemed silly to Jackson then and later. Perhaps
he was impetuous then. The whole army had to wait
at Vera Cruz for transport and supply. Tom Jackson
still had much to learn about patience.

His hardest lesson was at Jalapa, the first city up the steep road into the mountains toward Mexico City. There had been brisk fighting near by at the mountain pass of Cerro Gordo. But the road had to be held as well as taken. Jackson was detached from the advancing army to serve with the men left to guard the town. A young soldier less eager for a chance at military distinction might have found Jalapa a pleasant place. The natives were surprisingly friendly. The town was noted for its fine fruit, lovely flowers and its pretty girls, the "fair Jalapenas."

Even the impatient Jackson there began the serious study of the Spanish language in part at least with the "idea of making some lady acquaintances shortly." Still he was "mortified," he wrote, to be left behind while the Army, including many of his West Point associates, moved forward. The disappointment brought from him one of his first expressions of his faith that God orders all events.

"I throw myself in the hands of an all wise God," he wrote, "and hope it may yet be for the better. It may be His means of diminishing my excessive ambition; and after having accomplished His purpose, whatever it may be, He then in His infinite wisdom may gratify my desire."

As was always to be the case with the religious Jackson, he did not leave matters entirely in the hands of God. He learned that some new batteries of light artillery were to be formed. One was under the command of Captain John B. Magruder, a brave officer but such a tough taskmaster that most junior officers dodged service with him. Jackson sought it.

"I wanted to see active service, to be near the enemy in the fight," he said, "and when I heard that John Magruder had got his battery I bent all my energies to be with him, for I knew if any fighting was to be done, Magruder would be 'on hand.'"

Jackson was "on hand," too. On the road up and up from the sea he was praised and promoted again for gallant fighting at both Contreras and Churubusco. Then at the crucial battle of Chapultepec, in the final fighting for the capital, his performance awed even the daring Magruder. Furthermore, almost as if in a stadium, his courage was shown under the eyes of his top commanders.

The Mexican position before the advancing Americans seemed almost impregnable. The approaches to Mexico City were limited to narrow causeways across lakes and other difficult ground. A strong body of Mexicans attacked the infantry which Jackson was supporting. Mexican gunners in a fortified place opened murderous fire. The American infantry fell back before it, but Jackson raced forward looking for a good position for his guns. He found himself instead, as he described it later, on the unprotected road which was swept by cannons loaded with grape and canister shot and by bullets from the muskets of men in the Castle of Chapultepec above him.

One of his guns was quickly knocked out of action. Most of his horses were killed. His own men scattered and sought cover. Jackson looked for no shelter. He seemed careless of the bullets, walking up and down in front of the enemy's guns shouting defiance of danger to encourage his men.

"There is no danger," he yelled. "See! I am not hit."

Alone he pulled one of his guns into position. Then with the help of one sergeant, whose confidence had been restored by the officer's courage, Jackson began firing the cannon. It seemed a brave but futile enter-

Alone he pulled one of his guns into position

prise to the American general in command. He ordered Jackson to retire.

"I sent him back word," the young artilleryman said later, "that with one company of regulars as a support, I could carry the work, upon which he moved forward a whole brigade."

Magruder rode up, too. His horse was killed but he joined Jackson in firing the fieldpieces. Jackson's bravery was turning the tide of battle. The Mexicans fell back and this time Jackson led the pursuit which always seemed to him so essential a part of success. Attaching his guns to their wheels and axles, he hurried after the Mexicans retreating toward the San Cosme gate of the city. In his haste he got far ahead of most of the American troops.

Before him were only small detachments of Americans commanded by two of his West Point friends. These two Carolinians, Lieutenants Daniel Harvey Hill and Barnard E. Bee, were to be important in Jackson's life later. Far in advance of their own troops and confronted by a new stand of the Mexicans, it seemed doubtful that the two young officers and their men could survive. Then Jackson with his guns thundered up the narrow road to where they stood. Even the dashing Magruder counseled swift retreat, but the younger officers persuaded him to stand.

Down the road toward them charged 1,500 Mexican cavalrymen with their sabers shining in the sun. Only the narrow road and Jackson's coolness intervened to prevent their thundering purpose. As the cavalry in close array galloped toward the little force of Americans, he let go with his guns, tearing holes in the close-riding ranks of the Mexicans. Men and horses fell in heaps. The charge collapsed in bloody confusion. The surviving cavalrymen turned on the cluttered road in precipitate retreat. Jackson's guns blazed after them.

Other men fought bravely in that campaign. Other battles had to be won. But Jackson's bravery played a crucial part. Magruder gave him unstinted praise. So did his other superiors. He was promoted to the brevet rank of major. After the city had fallen he was asked if he had not been afraid as he received the concentrated fire of the Mexican forces.

"No," he said, "the only anxiety I felt was that I might not meet enough danger to make my conduct conspicuous."

The Lord had not diminished his ambition. Perhaps, as Jackson put it, He had gratified Jacksons' desire. Certainly the young lieutenant received almost embarrassing praise. Even General Scott, "Old Fuss and Feathers" himself, singled him out almost for public exhibition. At a reception the General gave for his victorious army, Scott stiffened in exaggerated sternness when Jackson came down the receiving line. He put his hands behind his back.

"I don't know that I shall shake hands with Mr. Jackson," he said in a voice that could be heard in the whole room.

Overcome with confusion, Jackson looked like an awkward boy again. And Scott waited till the attention of all present was centered upon the young, blushing officer before him. Then he went on.

"If you can forgive yourself for the way in which you slaughtered those poor Mexicans with your guns, I am not sure that I can."

Then warmly he shook Jackson's hand while laughter and applause rose around them. That was the highest praise possible. Others reflected the General's high

opinion. Even Mexicans, who forgave the young artilleryman's marksmanship when they discovered his gra-
cious manners, received him with cordiality. The Spanish he had begun to learn in Jalapa helped. In his spare
time as officer and gentleman he read, among other
books in Spanish, Lord Chesterfield's letters to his son
on the conduct of a gentleman. Tom was received, he
wrote home, by some of the oldest families of the
Mexican Republic. There is a suggestion in his letters
that he even considered marrying a lovely señorita and
remaining in Mexico. In grace and gallantry he was, in
the nine peaceful, pleasant months which he spent in
the high, beautiful Mexican capital, all that he had ever
hoped to be.

He came back to the United States on a troopship,
landing in New Orleans on July 17, 1848. He had his
picture taken there. In the daguerreotype, he seems the
very image of the dashing young soldier, slim, trim-
bearded. His uniform was tailored to perfection. Awkward young Tom seemed for the photographic moment
almost the dandy in arms. But he could never be quite
that. Despite the social graces he had shown in Mexico

City, he was still an earnest, reserved young man. Back home he found that not all remembered the recent war with a sense of military triumph. Many heroes had preceded him. Some people, particularly those who feared the extension of slavery, felt that the United States had robbed a neighbor by violence. Quarreling over slavery seemed more marked than celebration of conquest. Young Jackson was not involved in such debate.

His problems were personal. His service in war had pushed him up to the brevet (or honorary) rank of major in less than two years after his graduation. Before the war his great associate, Robert E. Lee, had still been a captain seventeen years after he left West Point. Now Jackson was back to his regular rank of first lieutenant in an army which had demobilized 140,000 men. People began to say, as one said in connection with Lieutenant Ulysses S. Grant, that army officers were idle loafers, doing nothing and living on the community. Instead, sometimes Jackson seemed over-anxious to do his duty as he saw it.

The path of glory seemed to lead not to lasting fame

but to a sort of dead end. Not military ambition, but problems of his physical and spiritual health occupied the Lieutenant's mind. He worried about his indigestion as he had never worried about danger in battle. He became increasingly interested in religion. In Mexico, he had shown brief interest in the Catholic Church. Less than a year after he came home he was baptized by an Episcopal minister, though he did not become a member of that church. Mentally and physically he seemed to move slowly in the stagnation of his career between wars. Finally, in Florida, where he was sent to duty at a backwoods post, he became involved in bickerings over military detail which seemed all that was left after military action.

Then he got a letter from Virginia. He had been recommended for the post of Professor of Natural and Experimental Philosophy and Artillery Tactics at the Virginia Military Institute by his old comrade in arms, Lieutenant Daniel Harvey Hill. In the dull years since they fought together far in front before Chapultepec, Hill, like many other officers, had resigned from the service. He had become Professor of Mathematics at

Washington College, located like V.M.I. in Lexington, Virginia. Before Jackson was chosen, many others had been mentioned for the position. His election seemed almost an accident. In his new mood, Jackson had the feeling that Providence had had a part in the matter.

4

"Hell & Thunder"

More young eyes looked sharply at Major Tom Jackson when he arrived at the Virginia Military Institute than had surveyed him when he first reached West Point. Even more than the United States Military Academy, the college at Lexington in the blue Virginia mountains embodied Southern cavalier ideas of pride and arms. Its students rejoiced in marching order but they had no greater love of stern discipline than most boys. They were ready to test quickly and, if possible, to haze a new professor. They had been waiting to get a look at Jackson.

Though Mexico was only three years behind the Major, memories of his gallantry there were fading. It would be ten years more before he saw action again. As he came to V.M.I. he was as aware of his short-comings as a teacher as he had once been of his weakness as a pupil. He had no doubts about teaching Artillery Tactics. He had learned that subject not only on the field but under fire as well. The other subject he was to teach, Experimental and Natural Philosophy which could be called General Science now, had been a difficult course for him at West Point. He had not studied it since. A friend asked him if he were not disturbed about teaching it.

"No," said the Major, then only twenty-seven years old but with a stern air which made him seem much older. "I can always keep a day or two ahead of the class. I can do whatever I will do."

He was going to have more trouble than he apparently thought keeping ahead of those boys from gay, rich, proud Virginia. That was evident the day he arrived. In the absence of the professor who regularly commanded the cadets, Jackson had been assigned to the command of the corps. The cadets knew he was coming but they did not know whether he would be on hand on the morning of August 14, 1851, when they assembled for the summer drill and encampment.

Other people had come to watch the cadets on the green parade ground in the midst of the blue mountains. Some were familiar folk. There were members of faculty families, townspeople, some of them girls. They made a little crowd under the shade of the trees at the edge of the parade ground when the band began to play and the cadets fell in. Then the erect, precise, young corps moved to the marching music. Suddenly above the blare of the band, a young, impertinent voice piped up.

"Come out of them boots," commanded the mocking voice. "They are not allowed in this camp."

From the smartly marching ranks came other comments. Student officers, including Cadet Adjutant Tom Munford, were shocked at such behavior. They were immediately aware that the object of the catcalls of the cadets was the new professor watching from the little crowd beside the field. They were also aware, as was the first cadet who shouted secretly from the ranks, that the officer's boots were enormous. And from his big feet, encased in worn but shining artillery boots, Major Jackson's whole figure seemed ludicrous to the critical cadets. He did not meet their pattern of military perfection. Indeed, in the exaggerated memories of that morning they recalled him later as looking more like a military scarecrow than a soldier. The double-breasted blue coat of his Virginia militia uniform, his white pants and white gloves, all looked too big for him. His very new-looking cap seemed ill-fitting, too, above his gaunt face.

Nobody even dreamed of calling him "Stonewall" then. Among the cadets, laughing behind his back, he was first to become "Fool Tom" and "Old Jack." Despite his earnest efforts to keep ahead of his students, he did not fool them in that process. He was not a good teacher. Even his fellow professors and his superior, the Superintendent, Colonel Francis H. Smith, admitted that after Jackson's military greatness was acclaimed.

The Major taught with a single-track rigidity the

The cadets called him "Fool Tom" and "Old Jack"

lessons he had drilled first into his own head. He taught science as if it were a field drill. Correct and courteous in his manner, he expected of cadets the discipline he demanded from himself and there were hardly any limits to that. He followed his ideas of duty to an extreme which made not only students but some of their elders think he was a crank. When once he arrived at the Superintendent's office a little early for an appointment, he stood in the rain until the exact moment came. He sweated in heavy uniform until the official order for change was formally posted. Cadets knew that he had a habit of standing facing the wall in his quarters concentrating on his studies and duties. And while the justice of his requirements of students was recognized, they regarded him as a bristling martinet. One wrote a verse comparing him with another teacher:

> The V.M.I., O what a spot,
> In winter cold, in summer hot.
> Great Lord Al . . . what a wonder,
> Major Jackson, Hell & Thunder.

Cadets not only laughed at his stern schedule, his big-booted measuring tread, his solemn silences, but they delighted in playing tricks on him. Some might have had serious results, as when a brick was dropped close to him from a third-story window. Jackson marched straight ahead, not even looking around. Some students wrote home saying only, "Old Jack skinned me." Others worked through the alumni seeking his dismissal. Among the hotheads was Cadet James A.

Walker, who so resented charges of misbehavior Jackson brought against him that he talked of a duel and muttered about assassination. Superintendent Smith sent Walker's father word to come and get his son before he became involved in serious trouble.

Yet despite the glum picture of Jackson painted in the memories of cadets, he was much respected in Lexington. He was, all agreed, a good man. He was as intense about his religion as his discipline. He came to his faith as slowly as to his learning. But when at last he joined the Presbyterian Church in Lexington, God became his commander never to be questioned. He entered church every time the doors opened. Some regulars in the other pews thought him a little queer because of the attentions he paid to a Sunday School for Negro children which he established. To the cadets, in addition to other names, he became "The Blue Light Deacon."

He was shy in society but welcome in it. Visiting was a popular pastime in those days and many doors were open to the serious Major. Young women as well as their elders liked him. Just two years after he came to Lexington, he married Elinor ("Ellie") Junkin.

She was the daughter of the president of adjacent Washington College which was later to become Washington and Lee after General Robert E. Lee closed his career there as its president. About a year after the wedding Jackson was a widower of thirty. Then, in 1857, he married again. This time his bride was Mary Anna (called Anna), one of the "fabulous Morrison girls" of North Carolina, three of whom married men who were to become famous Confederate generals. Both of Jackson's marriages were love affairs from beginning to end. It would have shocked cadets if they could have heard him using to his wives the Spanish words of endearment he had learned in romantic Mexico.

He seemed far from romantic to the boys. Apparently he enjoyed, as they did, annual visits of the corps to the fashionable Virginia springs, or watering places —Rockbridge Alum and Warm Springs. There the cadets in their smart uniforms met the crinolined belles of the South. But even on such occasions Old Jack was attentive to small details. He took pleasure in the precision of parade. He was at his best, so far as the boys were concerned, when he taught Artillery Tactics.

"When he would give the command to the cannoneers to fire," one recalled, "the ring of that voice was clear enough to be heard and to burn amid the rumbling of the wheels, giving life and nerve to the holder of the lanyard."

Obviously, as a man of such commanding voice shouting, "Ram home! Fire!" Jackson was happiest in his duty. He was training soldiers. It pleased him when his cadets were praised for their superior military qual-

Young women as well as their elders liked him

ities. That was particularly so when he led the cadet artillery to join other military organizations at the solemn occasion on December 2, 1859, when John Brown was hanged for seizing the Federal Arsenal at Harpers Ferry in an attempt to free the slaves. It is doubtful that Major Jackson realized that day how close at hand was the war for which in so many ways old John Brown pulled the firing cord. Jackson owned a slave or two. He believed in the rights of the States. But he regarded war as the "sum of all evils."

John Brown he regarded as a properly convicted criminal. Still, on the night before the hanging, Jackson prayed for Brown's soul though some of the cadets with whom he shared a crowded room smirked at the idea. And after he watched at close range the execution of that gaunt old insurrectionist against slavery, the Major reported with evident admiration that Brown "behaved with unflinching firmness" on the scaffold. He murmured another prayer as John Brown's body fell through the trap to eternity. As a Christian, Jackson feared that Brown might not be prepared to meet his Maker since he had refused to have a preacher with him. But if some of the cadets snickered at the hanging, Jackson watched Brown's conduct with respect. They were dissimilar men of very different ideas. Yet, in their notions about duty and devotion to it, much about them was the same.

"The wind blew his lifeless body to and fro," Jackson wrote at the end of his description of that solemn event. Greater winds were fanning the flames of fury between the North and the South. Jackson led his cadets back to Lexington by way of Richmond. He understood that "we have great reason for alarm, but my trust is in God." He did not believe, he wrote, that God would let the "madness of men" bring on a war. Back in Lexington he found, however, that the cadets showed an increasingly serious purpose in their artillery training. They marched with growing ardor and impatience. Jackson prayed for peace, but his class at V.M.I. tested a new type of rifled cannon and his report, late in 1860, persuaded Virginia to buy a dozen —just in case.

Then on Saturday, April 13, 1861, four days before Lincoln called for troops to invade the South and Virginia seceded from the Union, cadet impatience reached the fighting point at V.M.I. Many cadets in town for the Saturday holiday attended an exciting meeting on the courthouse grounds in Lexington. There, after much oratory, a secession flag was raised. Not all the sentiment was for war, however. The father of Jackson's first wife, soon to resign as president of Washington College, was an ardent abolitionist. Some citizens wanted to pull down the Rebel flag. One cadet got into a fight with a townsman. Other students and citizens became involved. The boys seemed to be getting the worst of it and a hurry call was sent back to the barracks for support. In quick response other cadets grabbed their muskets and headed for the town and the fight.

Only quick work by Superintendent Smith prevented a pitched battle. He headed off the cadets, got assurance from worried citizens that the townsfolk wanted no fighting, and led his reluctant boys back to the Institute. Far from satisfied and by no means silenced, the boys noisily greeted speeches to reprimand and quiet them. Disorder continued but it began to take on some qualities of a frolic. When Jackson came into the room where they were gathered, they were as ready for fun as a fight. In that spirit they greeted the cranky professor.

"Jackson! Jackson! Old Jack! Old Jack!" they shouted.

The tall, lean Major shook his head. Still they called for him. Then Superintendent Smith spoke to Jackson.

"I have driven in the nail," he said, "but it needs clinching. Speak with them."

Apparently Colonel Smith did not regard the demand for a speech from Jackson as a cadet joke. And Jackson always regarded a request from his superior as an order. He marched up to the platform in his big boots and faced the boys. He was in no joking mood. Boys who were there then remembered when they became old men how much taller than usual Old Jack looked and the blazing light in his eyes.

"Military men make short speeches," the stern professor said, "and as for myself I am no hand at speaking anyhow."

There were no snickers before him then. No calls came from the ranks of the listening cadets. They waited. The tall man before them was no awkward teacher. He was no longer the target of any prank or the hated disciplinarian. What he gave them was not reprimand but militant poetry.

"The time for war has not yet come," he told them, "but it will come, and that soon."

He must have paused then like a man ready to order a charge.

"And when it does come, my advice is to draw the sword and throw away the scabbard."

The whole room roared in a volley of respect.

5

Stone Wall

In command at Harpers Ferry sixteen days after Virginia seceded, Jackson still wore the plain blue uniform of a V.M.I. professor. No gold or insignia showed his rank as Colonel of Virginia volunteers. He was commonplace-looking alongside the brilliantly uniformed militia officers who had spent the first two weeks of war as if they were a holiday. Jackson put the celebrators to work. Parties attended by many visiting ladies ended. Incessant drills began. And Jackson began his famous career in strategy and tactics by kidnapping the rolling stock of a railroad.

It had taken some maneuvering before Jackson got his colonel's commission and his post at the town where John Brown had staged his raid and which now might be a gateway to the invasion of Virginia. In crowded, tumultuous Richmond he had almost been overlooked, his training and his Mexican War record forgotten. For a moment he seemed doomed to a desk job as a major of engineers. When friends intervened to insist upon assignment for him as a combat colonel, some hurrying politicians protested.

"Who is this Major Jackson?"

A delegate to the State Convention from the county in which V.M.I. is located answered promptly.

"He is one who, if you order him to hold a post, will never leave it alive to be occupied by the enemy."

He seemed to be assigned to just that sort of job at Harpers Ferry. But quickly he showed that his idea of holding a post was not merely occupying it. He went to work to make an army out of amateurs who were enthusiastic for war but not very eager for the discipline of arms. He worried his superiors in Richmond when he put cannon on the heights on the Maryland side of the Potomac. They feared such action might make Maryland join the Union side. Also, they insisted that the South was just defending itself, not attacking anybody else. With that attitude they would not even let Jackson tear up the tracks of the Baltimore & Ohio Railroad which tied the Union's East and West together and brought coal down from the mountains to the cities. So Jackson kidnapped the engines and cars.

First, he told the operators of the railroad that the coal trains coming down from the mountains disturbed his men at night and must be sent through at noon. The railroad people could hardly refuse such a request from the officer who controlled the bridge over the Potomac. Still, the empty cars went up at night and Jackson complained of them, too. So it was agreed that all trains would come through at the same daytime hours. Then when all came through at once, Jackson's men closed the line at each end, capturing fifty-six locomotives and three hundred cars. Unfortunately, before Jackson could devise ways to get the rolling stock south, he was relieved as commander by General

Joseph E. Johnston, who shared Richmond's caution. Johnston decided to evacuate Harpers Ferry. Jackson's captured trains were burned and run into the river.

In less than a month, however, Jackson had begun to make a disciplined force out of the dashing volunteers. General Johnston showed his confidence in him by making him commander of his First Brigade. It was composed of Virginians, most of them men from the Shenandoah Valley counties whom Jackson had been drilling hardest and upon whom he counted most. He called it a "promising brigade." Already they had the potentialities of the name they were soon to wear as the Stonewall Brigade. They showed those qualities first at a little place called Falling Waters where, though Jackson retreated according to orders, he badly mauled a much superior Federal force. The greater result was that the elderly Union General Robert Patterson lost his nerve and lost contact, too, with the Confederate forces he was supposed to keep from joining the main Confederate army between Washington and Richmond.

Jackson received his commission as brigadier general from General Robert E. Lee the day after the engagement at Falling Waters. Two weeks later the new General put his First Brigade on the march. The July day was hot and dusty. The men did not know where they were going. Jackson, as always, was as secretive as he was stern. That day even he did not know that he was on his way to acquire his famous name. From the direction of their march as indicated by the mountains, the men thought they were retreating. They moved in dispirited fashion. "Old Jack," as they had begun to call their commander in increasing confidence and affection, was not an inspiring sight. On his famous horse, Little Sorrel, which he had acquired at Harpers Ferry, his big boots almost dragged in the dust and the rim of his old gray cadet cap came far down on the bridge of his nose. He urged the lagging soldiers.

"Close up, men. Press on."

Still they lagged. Then Jackson called a halt. His adjutant read an order from General Johnston:

"Our gallant army under General Beauregard is now attacked by overwhelming numbers. The commanding general hopes that his troops will step out like men, and make a forced march to save the country."

There was a wild shout then. This was it. The plains of Manassas below Washington, where General Pierre

On his famous horse, Little Sorrel, Jackson

urged the lagging soldiers. "Close up, men. Press on."

Gustave Toutant Beauregard was attacked by Union General Irvin McDowell, were sixty tough, climbing miles away across the Blue Ridge. There the greatest armies ever assembled in America converged in battle. On the field, Beauregard's men were outnumbered. But behind Jackson's men, bluffed into immobility, was the Union force his brigade had slapped hard at Falling Waters. Slipping away, could the Confederate brigade reach Manassas on time?

The men stepped out. They seemed suddenly to become longer legged. Through the waters of the Shenandoah River they waded. Beyond they climbed the Blue Ridge in the dark at Ashby's Gap. Not until 2 A.M., after eighteen marching hours, was a halt called. All fell in their places in exhausted sleep except Jackson who, dispensing with sentries, watched over his men.

Crowds of people watched them pass in the morning, some of them wondering as the soldiers themselves did if they would reach the battle in time. Then, by one of the first such mechanized operations in warfare, the tired troops were hurried by railroad toward Manassas. They were gay in the hot cars but impatient. Jackson's infantry ("foot cavalry" they came to call themselves) got there on time. And in high spirits.

They were not alone in their high spirits. Other Southerners in arms had heard and believed that one Reb could beat ten Yankees. Also, many of the Union men they hurried to meet had similar ideas. Colonel (later General) William T. Sherman, who like Jackson had taught at a Southern military school before the war, understood that. His new soldiers in service on short enlistments, he said, "had been told often at home that all they had to do was to make a bold appearance, and the rebels would run."

That was the idea in Washington, too. Newspapers and politicians clamored, "On to Richmond." The North had the most men and equipment. The thing to do was to put down the rebellion promptly. Reluctant Union generals, aware of the lack of training of their men, could not secure delay. Indeed, if the Federal Army in the Valley of Virginia from which Johnston and Jackson had slipped away could have joined the Union forces at Manassas, together these Union forces would have been superior to any combination brought against them. They did not join each other. Confederate forces did. Even so, Union confidence in the army of General McDowell was sky-high. From Washington reporters and politicians, picnickers, and ladies in carriages with lunch boxes came to watch the spectacle. On both sides the war then seemed almost a summertime lark and each was sure that "our side" would quickly win.

Jackson's men, who had lengthened their stride in eagerness when they learned their destination, found themselves in the midst of confusion when they arrived. They were held in restive reserve. When things began to go wrong for the Confederates, they were still behind the lines. One of the first uses of semaphor signaling in battle brought the bad news to commanders that the Southerners had been outflanked on the left. Then, with the Federals threatening to turn both ends of their line, the Confederates broke. Fortunately, as they fell back in disorder, Jackson moved in with his First Brigade to occupy the "first favorable position for meeting the enemy." That place has been famous since as the Henry House Hill, named after the family of an old lady invalid there who was killed in the battle by a shell. It was there that Jackson encountered his old West Point classmate and Mexican War comrade, General Barnard E. Bee.

Bee was a brave man. A courtly South Carolinian, he came from a background unlike the mountain frontier in which Jackson was born. A perfect gentleman in arms, he had flashing black eyes and long black hair. He still wore a blue uniform, which was not strange on that field. Men in both armies wore a wide variety of uniforms—of different state and city military organizations. Men from the Deep South were vividly dressed. Some New York soldiers wore Turkish trousers and red fezzes. On the field were men in cock-feathered hats and English plaids. The blue and the gray had not become standardized. In his fine blue uniform, General Bee was sweating and desperate. Trying to rally his men, he waved the ornate sword given him by South Carolina for his services in the Mexican War. But he moaned to the plain, hard-chinned Jackson.

"General, they are beating us back."

Jackson's blue eyes were hard and cold.

"Sir," he said, "we'll give them the bayonet."

Jackson never had any picnic ideas about war. His First Brigade learned early that Old Jack liked cannon balls and cold steel. Those who faced him learned that, too. Now by the little stream Bull Run his eyes blazed like his batteries. He had more guns brought up. Up and down the line he rode in dramatic unconcern about the rifle bullets whistling around him. Careless of the fire, he directed and gestured with a hand wrapped in a handkerchief to cover a shrapnel wound. There was blood from his fingers to his elbow. His bravery as confident commander steadied his men. And General Bee, who died later in the action, rallied his men with an equal show of courage. He pointed to Jackson with his sword.

"Look!" he shouted to his South Carolinians. "There is Jackson standing like a stone wall. Let us determine to die here, and we will conquer. Follow me!"

Slowly, then faster and faster, the trend of the battle changed. Brave Union soldiers on the green and cluttered slopes of the Henry House Hill felt first the stiffening of the Confederate resistance. Then came the charge of Southerners with bare, gleaming bayonets upon the Federal lines. And the rebel steel moved forward accompanied by a high-pitched cry like that of fox hunters chasing their quarry. It resounds in history as the Rebel Yell. Jackson had waited coolly for the right moment in which to strike back.

"Hold your fire until they are on you," he ordered his men, "then fire and give them the bayonet. And when you charge, yell like furies."

Before the steel and the threatening scream the Yankees faltered, fell back in increasing disorder, then ran. Confederate cavalry and fresh artillery were brought up. Shells trailed the roads on which the Union soldiers moved. Before them the way was clogged by the wagons of supply and the carriages of spectators who had come out from Washington to see the sport and witness the expected victory.

A Confederate shell overturned a wagon on a narrow bridge. The retreat clotted into a panic. Out of Virginia, across the Potomac bridges, the broken pieces of the first great Federal army poured into the streets of the frightened capital. President Lincoln stayed up all night listening to the dark reports. And all night a

General Bee rallied his men. "Look!" he shouted.

"There is Jackson standing like a stone wall."

heavy rain fell upon the retreating and, as one observer said, "spongy-looking" soldiers. Washington was bogged in disaster and mud. Many hopelessly expected capture in the morning.

That, of course, did not happen. Perhaps it could not have been accomplished. No real pursuit followed the Federal stragglers clattering across the bridges. That was not Jackson's fault. After the battle, while surgeons were dressing the shattered middle finger of his wounded hand, dignified President Jefferson Davis of the Confederate States came on the scene. Pushing aside the doctors, Jackson cheered the President.

"Give me ten thousand men and I will be in Washington tonight," he promised.

His proposal was not accepted. The Confederacy had won a great victory but its armies were battered, too. Also, though that seemed silly to such an aggressive fighter as Jackson, the rigid President Davis still wanted to prove that the South was only defending its own land. Jackson believed from the beginning in striking fast, hard and where it would hurt. That seemed to him to be the plan of the Lord of Battles to whom he regularly gave credit for his victories. He did that after

this first battle of Manassas (or Bull Run, as it has become better known) though he expressed earthly satisfaction, too, in his feeling that "the First Brigade was
to our Army what the Imperial Guard was to the first
Napoleon."

Already the name and fame of "Stonewall" were
spreading. General Bee's sad friends in South Carolina
told the story of Jackson's stalwartness. Across the
South, eager for early victory, the tale was repeated and
reprinted. It seemed to fit Jackson's character and the
Confederacy's hopes then. But one who served with
him thought the nickname might better have been
"Thunderbolt," "Tornado," or "Hurricane." He was
the same old Jackson V.M.I. had known, nevertheless.
A few days after the battle Jackson's minister in Lexington received a letter addressed in the General's hand-
writing. He tore it open in the post office, promising
others there that here was real news of the big victory.
He read the letter which Jackson had written on the
morning after the battle:

In my tent last night, after a fatiguing day's service,
I remembered that I had failed to send you my contri-

bution to our colored Sunday School. Enclosed you will find my check for that object, which please acknowledge at your earliest convenience, and oblige

Yours faithfully,

T. J. JACKSON

6

"If the Valley Is Lost . . ."

The name "Stonewall" did not change Jackson. He worried because the idea of Confederate strength, implied in the nickname for him, spread across the South after the battle. Hailing one quick victory, Southerners got the notion of a short and easy war. Jackson knew better. Later he spoke of the over-confident months after Bull Run as the most disturbing period of the war.

He did not relax. In his camp not far from the battle-field, he drilled his men harder than ever. He denied furloughs. Some resented his sternness. Many more had pride in his command. The Brigade as a whole had affection for its commander. Even gay young officers in red and blue sashes, who liked apple brandy and the dancing girls, respected the General's almost religious sense of duty. If they sometimes mocked, they always approved his prayers. The four guns in one of the Brigade's artillery batteries were called Matthew, Mark, Luke and John. Men of the Stonewall Brigade said they spoke the true gospel.

Then suddenly the camp rumor spread that "Stonewall" and the Stonewall Brigade were to be separated. It was true. Jackson, made a major general, was to command all the Confederate forces in the Shenandoah Valley from which so many of his men came. They were to stay behind with the Army before Richmond. On November 4, 1861, the Brigade lined up in a rare and probably its last spit-and-polish parade for its General. In a clearing in a red autumn forest, the men waited in absolute silence when Jackson, in his rumpled uniform, rode up on Little Sorrel. He spoke slowly.

"Officers and men of the First Brigade, I am not here to make a speech but simply to say farewell."

His eyes swept along their silent ranks.

"I met you first at Harpers Ferry in the commencement of the war, and I cannot take leave of you without giving expression to my admiration of your conduct from that day to this, whether on the march, in the bivouac, the tented field, or on the bloody plains of Manassas, where you gained the well-deserved reputation of having decided the fate of the battle."

He went on in praise and farewell. Then something of the blaze which had marked his eyes in battle came into them again. Erect in his stirrups, he threw his reins aside, and his voice roared above the lines of men among the red trees.

"In the Shenandoah you were the First Brigade; in the Army of the Potomac you were the First Brigade; in the second corps of this army you are the First Brigade; you are the First Brigade in the affections of your general; and I hope by your future deeds and bearing you will be handed down to posterity as the First Brigade in our second War of Independence. Farewell!"

As he settled back into his saddle, a great yell rose

from the men. Suddenly Jackson seemed awkward again. Unable to hide his emotions, he waved his battered cap and galloped off.

Warm welcome waited him in Winchester, thirty miles up the valley from Harpers Ferry. The good, hospitable people along the Shenandoah regarded him as a valley man. They had sought Jackson as the protector of their pleasant towns, their fertile fields and their herds of cattle. The valley was worth protecting. It was both a grainery for the South and a gate into its heart. Green and tended, but steeply wild and rocky, too, the region extends 150 miles between the Allegheny and Blue Ridge mountains to the Shenandoah's meeting with the Potomac at Harpers Ferry, fifty miles from Washington. Part of it becomes two valleys where Massanutten Mountain rises abruptly to divide the Shenandoah into North and South Forks. Steep passes connected the two valleys. There were half-hidden and little-known roads. It was a scene for a defensive strategist, but a road for invaders, too.

Jackson could have had no more pleasant town for his headquarters than Winchester. He liked its warm-hearted people. They welcomed Jackson's well-loved

wife, Anna, who came up from North Carolina to visit
him there. They had a happy time in the house of a
Presbyterian minister with whom Jackson could talk

He would have amazed men who saw only his sternness

theology while he was secret about strategy. Sometimes
within the secrecy of the house, too, he played with
children in a manner which would have amazed men
who saw only the stern commander. But there was

little play connected with the job he had in the valley about the house.

"All the Confederate forces in the lower Shenandoah Valley" which he was to command turned out to be only a few badly organized, undisciplined companies of militia. With them he was supposed to guard the valley which constituted the left wing of the Confederate armies in Virginia. Also, he had to be ready to march east again to Manassas in case President Lincoln's new General George Brinton McClellan, who was building a new great army, should attack.

The driving drillmaster went to work again. This time, however, his toughest job was not training men to march and fight but making his colleagues and some of his superiors understand the business of fighting a war. His first problem was reduced when, to the mutual delight of men and commander, his old Stonewall Brigade was ordered to join him at Winchester. Jackson's greater difficulty was with politicians, not soldiers.

When the Stonewall Brigade arrived he had a total of 4,000 men while the Federals had about 50,000 men pressing on his position. Fortunately they were scattered. Jackson, whose idea of protecting was attacking, decided to hit first at the village of Romney. That was thirty-five miles away on the south branch of the Potomac, held by 5,000 Union soldiers. Its capture would drive a wedge between Federal armies in the area. More important, a movement toward Romney might make McClellan think the army before him in eastern Virginia was weakened by forces absent in the west and tempt him to attack before he was ready. To carry out this plan, Jackson was sent 6,000 men under General William W. Loring. They arrived on a sunny Christmas Day. On New Year's Day Jackson moved.

The day was like spring. Warm weather had kept the grass green. Forsythia bushes were blooming. In the unseasonable heat untrained men threw their overcoats and blankets away. Next day it rained as they marched. Then the rain turned to sleet. Cold winds blew. Men and horses slipped on frozen mountain roads. From horses' knees hung bloody icicles. Men slept in the snow. Grumbling mounted among the men, particularly in Loring's badly disciplined division. Apparently Loring, who had outranked Jackson in the old army, encouraged the complaints of his soldiers. In a near mutiny the curses grew that Jackson was a crazy man on an insane errand. Jackson shared the hardship. Cursing men were surprised when, in the icy dawn, he rose beside them in snowy fields. He pressed on, and on January 14, 1862, marched into Romney from which the enemy had fled. Stonewall decided to let Loring's force remain to occupy the important outpost. Perhaps that was a position of honor. Loring didn't like it. And he did not keep that feeling to himself.

Six days after Jackson got back to Winchester he received a sharp message from Secretary of War Judah P. Benjamin: "Our news indicates that a movement is making to cut off General Loring's command; order him back immediately."

All Jackson's work was undone. Like a good soldier he carried out Benjamin's order. Also, he sent the Secretary of War his resignation. The news caused an explosion in Winchester and Richmond. General Johnston, who first knew of Benjamin's order when he got Jackson's letter, did not like being by-passed. He was shocked by Benjamin's interference with field operations. Still he wrote Jackson that "the danger in which our very existence as an independent people lies, requires sacrifices from us all who have been educated as soldiers."

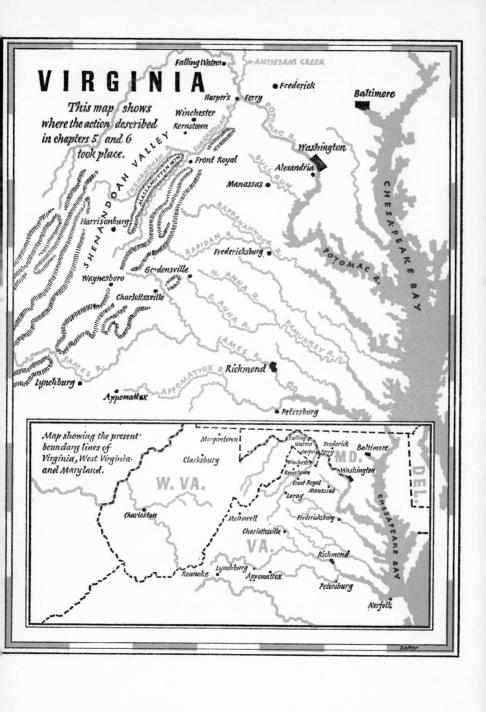

VIRGINIA

This map shows where the action described in chapters 5 and 6 took place.

Falling Waters
ANTIETAM CREEK
Frederick
Harper's Ferry
Baltimore
Winchester
Kernstown
Washington
SHENANDOAH VALLEY
Front Royal
Alexandria
MASSANUTTEN MTS.
BULL RUN
Manassas
Harrisonburg
RAPPAHANNOCK R.
POTOMAC R.
RAPIDAN R.
Waynesboro
Gordonsville
Fredericksburg
CHESAPEAKE BAY
N. ANNA R.
Charlottesville
S. ANNA R.
PAMUNKEY R.
JAMES R.
JAMES R.
Richmond
Lynchburg
APPOMATTOX R.
Appomattox
Petersburg

Map showing the present boundary lines of Virginia, West Virginia and Maryland.

Morgantown
Falling Waters
Frederick
Baltimore
Clarksburg
Harper's Ferry
Winchester
MD.
W. VA.
Kernstown
Washington
Front Royal
DEL.
Luray
Manassas
Charleston
McDowell
Fredericksburg
CHESAPEAKE BAY
Charlottesville
VA.
Richmond
Roanoke
Lynchburg
Petersburg
Appomattox
Norfolk

Salter

"Sacrifices!" Jackson roared in response. "Have I not made them . . . Nor shall I ever withhold sacrifices from my country, where they will avail anything. I intend to serve here, anywhere, in any way I can, even if it be as a private soldier. But if this method of making war is to prevail, the country is ruined."

Jackson's resignation was not accepted. But he carried his point. He was ready to labor with untrained subordinates. He was prepared to accept the orders of his superiors. He could not, however, dismiss the danger of political meddling in military operations in the field. Perhaps he did not realize then how much of the South's hope would depend upon similar meddling on the Union side. The South could not risk such amateur interventions.

General McClellan with a great new Union Army was ready to move again. Before overwhelming numbers, General Johnston had to fall back from Manassas to prevent McClellan from getting between him and the Confederate capital. Then, on February 27, General Nathaniel Banks, as a part of the same general Union movement, crossed the Potomac River at Harpers Ferry with 38,000 men and eighty guns. Jackson was expected to fall back as part of a general defense. Instead, he asked permission to hold his ground. Far from retreating, he marched his smaller force out to meet Banks who moved cautiously, believing exaggerated reports as to Jackson's strength. The Confederate offered Banks two opportunities to attack him. The Union general declined.

"If this valley is lost," Jackson wrote to a friend in Richmond at the time, "Virginia is lost." And the clear, unstated conclusion also was that the Confederacy would be lost.

Yet it seemed apparent that Jackson would have to abandon pleasant Winchester. People could hear the rumble of departing baggage wagons. Jackson did not seem to be disturbed. He told the Presbyterian preacher with whom he lived that he expected to dine there on the following evening. He expressed the view that "by the vigorous use of the bayonet and the help of divine Providence" he could defeat Banks. He had expected to withdraw his men a few miles south of Winchester and then return to fall on Banks' inexperienced men as they entered Winchester in the dawn.

When he held a council of war with his officers,

however, he found that someone had blundered. The infantry had followed the baggage wagons so far south that they had been marched out of the possibility of any return for a dawn attack. Stonewall was furious, yet there was nothing to do but follow after his men. He left late, riding with young Dr. Hunter McGuire, the medical chief of his forces. As they looked back on the town McGuire saw that Jackson's face was contorted in a violent rage.

"That is the last council of war I will ever hold," he said. It was.

Banks occupied Winchester in the morning. In a few days that Union general, who had been a prominent Massachusetts politician, hoped that he might co-operate with the great Federal army before Richmond. Indeed, Colonel Turner Ashby, on March 21, gave Jackson information which indicated that Banks' army was leaving. Though Ashby failed to discipline his men as Jackson required, the General had great admiration for him. That dashing cavalry leader did not often make mistakes in information. He personified the symbol of the mounted knight in the romantic South. He rode like the wind and fought like the devil. One of his men, whose discipline never quite matched their daring, said, "We thought no more of riding through the enemy's bivouac than of riding around our father's barn." They brought back facts and prisoners. This time, however, Ashby's information was wrong.

On Sunday morning, March 22, Stonewall moved boldly forward to join Ashby. His men had marched more than twenty miles the day before. They were dog-tired when Jackson sent them into what he thought was a little skirmish at Kernstown, a village four miles south of Winchester. Stonewall expected little trouble. His men moved in briskly. Then he saw them falter. He found that he faced not just a few companies but a first wave of 3,000 Yankees who hurled themselves in a violent counterstroke at the tired Southerners. Behind them was the whole division of General James Shields in command of Banks' advance force. With 9,000 men he had been waiting for Jackson there. Through the crumbling Confederate line, Jackson rushed furiously to the front. Even his Stonewall Brigade was retreating, an incident for which he never forgave its commander.

Stonewall seized a small drummer boy. "Beat the

rally," he told him. Under Stonewall's eyes the boy beat as he had never done before. But the men seemed not to hear. Reluctantly Jackson fell back. Outnumbered as he was, however, he covered his retreat with such a show of force that Shields did not closely pursue him. The defeat might have strengthened Jackson in his feeling about fighting on the Sabbath Day. Yet immediately after Kernstown he seemed singularly undisturbed. One of Ashby's cocky young cavalrymen found the General standing by a fence-rail fire.

"The Yankees don't seem willing to quit Winchester, General!"

Jackson was not bothered by the brash boy. "Winchester is a very pleasant place to stay in, sir."

The cavalryman grinned. "They said the Yankees were retreating, but I guess they're retreating after us."

Moodily Jackson regarded the fire. "I think I may say I am satisfied, sir."

More formally he expressed that view in his report of the defeat to General Johnston: "This fight will probably delay, if not prevent, their [the Yankees] leaving and I hope will retain others."

It did just that. General Shields was convinced Jackson would not have hit him so boldly if he had not had large reinforcements behind him. Banks telegraphed to Washington reports exaggerating Jackson's force of scarcely 3,000 effectives to 15,000 men, then (though he said he didn't believe it) to 30,000. When President Lincoln got the news he stopped the reinforcement of McClellan and took valley forces away from his command. On the eve of his planned attack on Richmond, McClellan found his army suddenly reduced by 50,000 men. His operations were suspended.

The true meaning of Jackson's defeat became clear. Hardly any army derived greater benefit from taking a beating. The Confederate Congress formally passed a resolution thanking him. Better still, in a heartened Virginia recruits began to come in. Jackson hoped that he would never have to fight a battle on Sunday again, but from Kernstown on if fighting was required on the Sabbath his conscience was not troubled by it. Now he had Richmond's thanks and he and Lee fashioned an effective strategy based as much on Washington's fears as the terrain of the valley.

7

Hide and Seek

To lively band music, on May 20, 1862, General Richard Taylor marched his brigade of spick-and-span Louisiana troops up the Valley Pike to New Market. There the handsome son of President Zachary Taylor found Stonewall sitting on a rail fence sucking a lemon. Jackson had watched the parade of Taylor's Irish and French Creole soldiers as they approached from the command of General Richard S. Ewell who had been sent to reinforce the valley troops. Moving

jauntily in fresh gray uniforms and immaculate gait-
ers, they seemed picture-book soldiers beside Jackson's gawking men. In comparison Stonewall's ragamuffin regiments looked like a mob in arms.

Jackson, as Taylor first saw him, was little more impressive. The Louisiana officer never forgot his first
sight of Jackson's "cavalry boots covering feet of enormous size" nor his "mangy cap with vizor drawn low,
a heavy dark beard, and weary eyes." Jackson lowered
the lemon. His men were accustomed to the combination of Jackson and his favorite fruit. Taylor watched
the slow gesture Stonewall made with the lemon as he
inquired the road and distance the Louisiana men had
marched that day.

"Keazletown road, six and twenty miles."

"You seem to have no stragglers," the lemon-sucking
General said.

"Never allow straggling," Taylor said with pride.

"You must teach my people; they straggle badly."

Near them Taylor's Creole band struck up a waltz.
Jackson sucked thoughtfully, then commented.

"Thoughtless fellows for serious work," he said.

Taylor defended the gay appearance of his men and

withdrew. Jackson paid more attention later that day
when another soldier came on a sweating horse from
Ewell's command. He brought Jackson the news that
neither the Louisiana troops nor any other reinforcements might be available for the great valley campaign
which Stonewall had been planning while he sucked
his lemon on the fence.

This was a crucial day at the end of a difficult time.
Nearly two months before when he retreated from
Kernstown, Jackson had relieved the pressure of Mc-
Clellan on Richmond. Great dangers plagued him still.
Around his little force of 4,000 hard-hit men when he
retreated down the valley was the cautious Banks. To
the west were the forces under John C. Frémont, famous explorer and Presidential candidate. On the east
was General Shields who, having beaten Jackson once,
figured he could do it again. Together they had ten
times as many men as Jackson. Stonewall did not mean
to let them attack him together. Fortunately for him,
reassured officials in Washington, with their eyes again
on Richmond, planned no joint action against him.

Jackson's weakness seemed to justify Yankee confidence. His men were so poorly armed that he asked

for pikes if he could not be supplied with guns. Again he set about making the most effective force of the men he had. Some of the best men he had gave him trouble. Jackson almost lost the services of the popular, dashing Colonel Ashby. He threatened to resign when the General insisted that Ashby's cavalry of gentlemen hunters, who wanted to fight a war like a fox hunt, be organized and disciplined as soldiers. Even a regiment of the Stonewall Brigade, its enlistment for a year having expired, demanded its discharge. With no hesitation Jackson invoked the new Confederate Conscription Law.

"Tell the colonel he need not ask me how to deal with mutineers," he said. "Shoot them where they stand."

He meant it, too. A chaplain intervened for three recruits sentenced to be shot for deserting to the enemy.

"Do you know you are sending these men's souls to hell?" the chaplain asked Jackson.

Jackson was in no mood then to discuss theology. He took the chaplain by the shoulders and threw him out of his tent. Others thought they were roughly treated, too. And Jackson's secretiveness about his plans

galled General Ewell, who had been sent on a tempo-
rary basis to help him and fought gallantly with him.
The bald, pop-eyed, cursing Ewell had very little interest in religion, which was always so important to
Jackson. As an always eager fighter, he felt that he
should be informed about fighting plans. Ewell was
using his mildest language when he called Jackson an
"enthusiastic fanatic" and "this old fool."

Jackson's chief quartermaster, who had to carry out
the General's often perplexing orders about the movement of his supply wagons, declared that "we are in
great danger from our crack-brained General." Others
got the same impression when Jackson led his men east,
then west, along bad roads and apparently around in
circles. The process bewildered General Banks, too. He
sent word to his superiors that Jackson had crossed the
Blue Ridge and abandoned the valley. Therefore he
suggested that he move to the support of McClellan.
"Such an order would electrify my force," he said.
Some electrification awaited him.

"Always mystify, mislead and surprise the enemy,"
Jackson said. But sometimes his own followers felt that
they were mystified first.

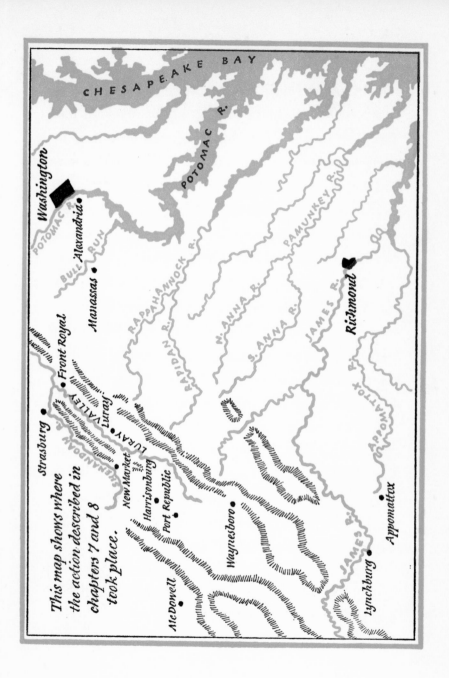

This map shows where the action described in chapters 7 and 8 took place.

His men were confused and citizens of the valley thought that he had disappeared. He arrived suddenly in Staunton at the head of the valley and was as suddenly gone again. While there a leading citizen, eager for the town's defense, asked his plans.

"Judge Baldwin, can you keep a secret?" Jackson asked.

"Certainly, General. Certainly."

"Well, so can I."

He was gone again. A variety of rumors spread about his movements. One which worried Federal authorities in Washington was that he had crossed the Potomac high up that stream and was moving through Maryland on Washington. The truth came on May 9, from the village of McDowell, West Virginia, on the far western edge of the valley. There Jackson had hit the advance troops of Frémont's forces on Bull Pasture Mountain the day before.

"God blessed our arms with victory at McDowell yesterday," Jackson telegraphed.

One of the three forces against him had been hit and pushed back in retreat. Two more remained when Jackson got back to the valley where he had left Ewell on guard. He had barely returned before he received a letter from General Lee.

"Whatever movement you make against Banks," Lee told him, "do it speedily, and if successful drive him back toward the Potomac, and create the impression, as far as possible, that you design threatening on that line." Lee also told him, "If you can use General Ewell's division in an attack on Banks it will prove a great relief to the pressure on Fredericksburg."

Lee and Jackson understood each other. Stonewall said that he would follow Lee blindfolded. Both knew that in Washington there was new expectation of the fall of Richmond. Indeed, McClellan's troops could be seen from the steeples of the Southern capital. Above Richmond, about to join McClellan, was a fine new army under General McDowell to which, as fears of Jackson subsided, were added some Federal troops from the valley. President Lincoln planned to go to Fredericksburg on May 26, to review McDowell's army. That date was set for six days after General Taylor led his snappy Louisiana men to the meeting with Jackson on the valley turnpike near New Market.

The hard-riding courier who followed Taylor to

New Market that day brought bitter news. General Johnston, wanting every man he could get to defend Richmond, had ordered Ewell to come east. Johnston's order vetoed any notion of an attack on Banks. Yet Jackson knew that, with Frémont and Banks separated and troops under General Shields moved to the army before Richmond, the time was ripe to carry out the Jackson-Lee plan to drive Banks toward the Potomac. Ewell agreed to delay on Johnston's order until Jackson could appeal to Lee. By nightfall the news came that Ewell's men could stay. In the dawn Jackson's offensive began.

It seemed like a strange offensive to many of Stonewall's marching men. Taylor's Louisiana brigade had marched around the southern end of Massanutten Mountain from Luray Valley into the main valley. They had marched down the valley with bands playing loud enough to be heard by the deafest of Banks' spies. Then suddenly Jackson's army turned and crossed the mountain into the Luray Valley from which Taylor had come. The movement, however, united all of Jackson's forces, now increased to 16,000 men. In the Luray Valley his movements were completely screened as he moved secretly toward his first objective, the town of Front Royal. It lay in a small valley near the meeting of the two branches of the Shenandoah River. There a Union garrison guarded the flank of Banks' main force at Strasburg, ten miles away. As they approached, a young woman, Belle Boyd, a famous Confederate spy, came out with the news that less than a thousand men held the place.

Completely surprised, the small Union garrison fought bravely. They upset Jackson's timetable. Off guard and overwhelmed, however, they were routed. Only 400 of the 1,000 Yankees there escaped. And one who did escape was not believed when he rushed into Banks' headquarters at Strasburg two hours later. Obviously what he reported was only a cavalry raid. Banks was sure that Jackson was still far up the valley. The political General rejected reports.

"By God, sir, I will not retreat. We have more to fear, sir, from the opinions of our friends than from the bayonets of our enemies."

When he did move, however, fear well served speed. Ashby's spirited cavalry wrought havoc with Banks' rear guard, but the lack of discipline of which Jackson complained showed itself among the horsemen again. They stopped to loot the richly loaded wagons of the Yankees. While they gorged themselves on fine food and loaded themselves with loot, Banks' army reached Winchester. A chance to destroy the army on the road had been lost.

Next morning 10,000 Confederate bayonets glimmered around the town. But no easy task awaited them. The town was courageously defended. Jackson had driven his men hard in the pursuit. On the night they approached the town a colonel had suggested that his men be allowed to halt for a rest.

"Colonel," Jackson told him, "I yield to no man in sympathy for the gallant men under my command; but I am obliged to sweat them tonight to save their blood tomorrow. The line of hills southwest of Winchester must not be occupied by the enemy's artillery. My own must be there and in position by daylight."

The battle of Winchester depended upon the possession of those hills. As the fighting hung in the balance, Stonewall came upon General Taylor leading his men whose jaunty march to music had made them seem to Jackson "thoughtless fellows for serious work."

"General," Jackson asked, "can your brigade charge a battery?"

"It can try."

The brigade moved into a brutal fire. Some of the men began to duck.

"What are you dodging for?" Taylor shouted to his men. "If there is any more of it, you will be halted under this fire for an hour."

Then as the men leaped to the charge Taylor was aware of Jackson in the exposed position beside him. Stonewall looked reproachful.

"I am afraid you are a wicked fellow," he said. But as Taylor's men drove the Yankees from their position, Jackson on Little Sorrel waved his cap in the air. "Now let's holler," he cried.

Back through Winchester poured the beaten Federal troops. Jackson had the chance he had sought to pursue and destroy the routed army. Never, he said later, had he seen a time when it was in the power of the cavalry "to reap a richer harvest of the fruits of victory." Ashby's dashing but undisciplined men were not at hand.

Banks got away. But across the Potomac, where Banks had gone, panic spread. The grand review of

Belle Boyd, a Confederate spy, gave them some news

McDowell's army was postponed. Lincoln ordered McDowell "to halt the movement on Richmond, to put 20,000 men in motion at once for the Shenandoah." Under Shields they marched to meet Frémont's forces from the west to pin Jackson in a tight place along the Potomac and prevent his retreat up the valley. In triumph Jackson seemed also in a trap.

Among old friends in Winchester Stonewall did not seem disturbed. His men, resting in the pleasant town, enjoyed the rich rations left by the Union General whom they promptly christened "Commissary Banks." Though they were surrounded by three armies and 60,000 men, all talk of Jackson as "crack-brained" subsided.

"Old Jack got us into this fix, and with the blessing of God he will get us out of it."

8

Double Play

Jackson moved. He seemed less concerned than his men about the greater armies on each of his flanks. The ragged but unusually well-fed men made a joke about his problems. They said that Stonewall's greatest concern was getting safely south a double line of wagons eight miles long because of the well-loved lemons contained among the stores he had seized. Nobody knew better than Jackson, however, that the time for prudence had come, or that the situation was, as President Lincoln put it at the time, "a question of legs." Stonewall's infantry had not become "foot cavalry" for nothing.

Lincoln seemed to get first jump. In fury Jackson learned that the colonel of a force he had left to guard Front Royal had let the Yankees capture the town. He confronted its defeated commander.

"How many men did you have killed, Colonel?"

"None."

"And how many wounded?"

"None."

Something like his battle fury showed in Jackson's eyes. "Do you call that a fight, man? You're under arrest."

He could not so sternly or easily dismiss the problem of escape. The Union President's plan "to throw Frémont's force & part of McDowell's" in Stonewall's rear was proceeding rapidly. Furthermore, when Front Royal fell, the Stonewall Brigade was farther down the valley near Harpers Ferry. Even if the main body of Jackson's army could slip down the valley before the Union armies joined, it seemed doubtful that the Stone-

"Do you call that a fight, man? You're under arrest."

wall Brigade could make it in time. As they hurried back to join the main army there was muttering among the Stonewall men. Jackson always gave them the tough and dirty jobs. They were to be lost in his crazy movements. Instead, at the end of an all-night, thirty-six-mile march, they came up to find Jackson fighting to hold the road open for them. Frémont was held back. He did not seem as eager as Mr. Lincoln wanted him to be for a fight. The gate Lincoln had planned never closed and Stonewall with all his army moved up the valley.

The question of legs was still not settled. In the main valley as Jackson moved up it, Frémont followed him just across the Shenandoah River. Beyond Massanutten Mountain, Shields' troops hurried down the Luray Valley. At any time Frémont might get across the river. Shields could bring his troops across the mountain. And both valleys came together, as the Union troops might do also, at a little town called Port Republic on a peninsula between the North and South Forks of the Shenandoah. At any point along the way the Union troops might unite. The geography of the valley upon which Jackson so much depended seemed to promise that his retreat only led certainly to the meeting of the superior Union forces against him.

Jackson's situation, as the Union commanders saw it, was like that of a fugitive pursued by the police who were driving him inevitably to a corner. His pursuers shouted their confidence after him as they chased him.

"I hope you will thunder down on his rear," General Shields said in a dispatch to Frémont. "I think Jackson is caught this time."

With such superior forces on each of his flanks, Jackson pressed on. Frémont had been only three miles to the west when the Confederates marched out of Strasburg. A storm pelted them, as they hurried up the valley, with hailstones as big as walnuts. In a cold, driving rain men fell exhausted.

"Press on, men, press on. Close up, men. Close up," Jackson commanded along the column. He threatened to remove officers who could not keep their exhausted men on the march. He himself saw to it that bridges were burned so that General Shields could not cross Massanutten Mountain from Luray Valley to strike him from the east as Frémont threatened him on the west. And Providence, upon whom he so often counted, seemed to help him when the Shenandoah flooded twelve feet in four hours and washed away pontoons on which Frémont planned to cross the Shenandoah.

All the way Ashby's men harried and held back the van of Frémont's forces. Yet the dangers which dogged the valley army on this march seemed marked with special ill omen when Ashby, who had seemed so in-vulnerable as to be almost immortal, fell shot through the heart. The news shook Stonewall. Though Ashby's failure to discipline his men sometimes infuriated Jackson, he shared the general admiration for him as an almost legendary warrior. And his death could hardly have come at a time when he was needed more.

Jackson received the news as he approached the end of his retreat near Port Republic. There, where he could watch the two arms of the valley, a few miles southeast of the site of an old inn called the Cross Keys, he had counted on Ashby's swift, daring activity. After hearing that Ashby had fallen he wrote a eulogy in his official report: "His daring was proverbial, his powers of endurance almost incredible, his character heroic, and his sagacity almost intuitive." Jackson put no pretense in those phrases. Yet at a time when he needed Ashby's swift daring between the two Union armies, he understood that the war was no longer one which individual valor could win, nor the death of a brave man lose.

The next day, Saturday, June 7, Stonewall was ready. He invited attack by Frémont on his army under Ewell at Cross Keys, but the Union forces seemed timid. Next morning, however, though Jackson said he hoped there would be no battle on the Sabbath Day, the sound of cannonading to the northwest told Jackson at Port Republic that Frémont had engaged Ewell.

"Major," Jackson said to the Rev. Robert L. Dabney, a Presbyterian minister who had the military rank as a member of his fighting staff, "wouldn't it be a blessed thing if God would give us a glorious victory today."

What Stonewall had prepared was two victories, two battles in which he could defeat separately and one at a time both his adversaries on almost the same ground. Much undoubtedly in so intricate a business depended on Providence. General Ewell, however, who was handling the fighting at Cross Keys, did not put his confidence in such a high power. Perhaps he stated a belief which endeared him to Jackson when he declared that "the road to glory cannot be traveled with much baggage." With or without the aid of Providence, Ewell was getting the better of Frémont who used his superior forces too cautiously. More than twice as many Yankees as rebels were killed. And when Frémont fell back late in the evening, Jackson put into operation his plan to pull most of his men under Ewell across the river to fight Shields who was threatening Port Republic.

Stonewall left a single brigade to hold back Fré-

A storm pelted them as they hurried up the valley

mont's army, saying that "by the blessing of Providence" he hoped to be back on that field at ten o'clock the next morning. His hopes were too high. Shields really meant it when he reported that he was "thundering down on Jackson's rear." He wrote the officer of his advance guard, "No man has had such a chance since the war commenced." And though he had spread his division out thin along the Luray Valley, he counted on catching the most feared Confederate. The Union forces had seized the steep, wooded hills about the battleground at Port Republic. Before the Yankee guns the Stonewall Brigade charged first and faltered. Jackson himself galloped toward them.

"The Stonewall Brigade never retreats," he shouted. "Follow me."

As always he was careless of the fierce fire around him. Still the going was tough and bloody for the Confederates until the dependable Taylor with his "thoughtless fellows" at great loss fought their way around and up to take the Union battery from the rear. Jackson was not going to be able to make his ten o'clock date with the small force he had left to hold Frémont. That

Union commander could hear the sounds of the battle at Port Republic. There was danger that he might fight his way through and effect the very juncture of the Union forces which Jackson had devised his battle to prevent. Delaying no longer, Stonewall sent orders for the small force holding Frémont to fall back and burn behind them the bridge which provided the only way to the Port Republic battle as they came.

Beyond the destroyed bridge this force joined in the defeat of Shields' men. Safe from the forces of Frémont, Jackson's soldiers set out to dispose of Shields. Across the river all the abandoned and baffled Frémont could do was to throw shells to the shore. Many of them fell among ambulances gathering up the many wounded of both armies. The Rebels thought poetic justice was done when a shell hit an ambulance with a Confederate and a Union soldier in it, missing the Confederate entirely and killing the Yankee outright.

Jackson's cavalry rode hard after Shields' men who were escaping down the Luray Valley. Pressed by his own fears, Frémont retreated down the main valley to Harrisonburg; then he abandoned that town, leaving large supplies. Six days after the battle he was back at Strasburg where the confident pursuit of Jackson had begun. Shields, too, was back in Front Royal. Beyond them in the North the image of Jackson grew as the invulnerable enemy. And in the South the news of his great valley campaign heartened a people no longer so self-confident as they had been after the first battle of Manassas.

With his little band Jackson had swept the valley region, always fighting against potentially stronger foes. In six weeks his men had marched 400 miles. They had beaten four Union armies, and fought five pitched battles in addition to almost daily skirmishes. They had captured 4,000 prisoners and vast amounts of stores—including plenty of lemons. As they rested at last, they little resembled the Southern knights pictured in romantic notions about war. Not much could be said for their uniforms except in terms of their variety and the ingenuity with which many of them were held together with rags and rope. Naked feet showed through ragged boots. But as the men of Stonewall they had held 175,000 Yankees in two great armies paralyzed before Richmond and Petersburg. It seemed to more people than Jackson

As they rested, they little resembled Southern knights

himself that Providence must have marched with so few in accomplishing so much. Stonewall himself was sure of it.

"General," he said, putting his arm around the shoulders of the irreligious but almost irresistible Ewell, "he who does not see the hand of God in this is blind, sir, blind!"

Old "Baldy" Ewell was not given to pious expression. He uttered more profanity than prayers. He was like another Virginia general who, rebuked by General Lee for swearing, replied, "General, you and Jackson do all the prayin' for the whole Army of Northern Virginia, but in heaven's name let me do the cussin' for one small brigade." Ewell no longer fumed, however, at Jackson's crazy ways. As a fighting man, he no longer questioned Stonewall's leadership. Of Jackson's fighting faith he had no doubts.

"If that be religion," he said of Jackson's powers with the aid of Providence about this time, "I must have it."

Both were going to need it.

9

The Seven Days

I f my coat knew my plans," Stonewall said, "I would take it off and burn it."

The secrecy and mystification with which his operations were surrounded seemed to increase after Port Republic. On June 12, 1862, he marched his men westward in an apparent pursuit of Frémont, then let them rest at the village of Mount Meridian on the Shenandoah. While they slept and bathed and patched their ragged clothes, Jackson worked at the business of deceiving his own army as well as the enemy, his officers as well as citizens of the region.

Evidence was scattered indicating that he was preparing for an advance to the north, perhaps into Maryland and Pennsylvania. In besieged Richmond the Georgia troops of General W. H. C. Whiting and General Alexander R. Lawton were ostentatiously entrained to reinforce him in plain view of a body of Union prisoners soon to be released. The prisoners could be counted on to spread reports. Still his own soldiers were confused. General Whiting, after Jackson had marched and countermarched his men, gave it as his opinion that Stonewall "hasn't any more sense than my horse."

Jackson was not disturbed by such opinions. He seemed almost to seek them. But in these crowded days after the end of his famous valley campaign, the secretive valley chieftain was going to have to learn his hardest lesson. He had trained undisciplined volunteers into a valiant army. He had threatened to resign in order to teach politicians not to meddle with his military movements. He had insisted upon discipline even from such idealized individualists as the lamented Ashby.

And since he had done so much himself, Providence had blessed his arms. Now he was going to have to learn that not even Stonewall himself could disregard the rules Providence set for other men.

The General disappeared from his army. Though he shared the news with no one else, the day before he moved from Port Republic he received a letter from General Lee, who had succeeded to the command of the armies in Virginia. Lee expressed the "liveliest joy" in Jackson's victories and outlined a greater plan to hit piecemeal McClellan's army divided by the Chickahominy River above Richmond. It was the kind of plan involving risk and reward which Jackson liked. He spread his rumors and prepared his men. Then, on June 21, he set out for a secret farmhouse rendezvous near Richmond for Lee's final briefing. He came part of the way in a closed mail car. Then he was in saddle fourteen hours and fifty miles.

Lee's plan was audacious. McClellan, who kept asking for more soldiers, had so many then that President Lincoln said that if he gave him more there would not be room for them to lie down and they would have to sleep standing up. Lee knew that to beat such an army he had to fight as Jackson had fought in the valley. He was ready to take the chance. Leaving Richmond thinly defended before McClellan's threatening army, he planned to destroy the Union General's exposed right wing north of the swampy Chickahominy River. Then, on McClellan's flank, he proposed to drive the Yankee leader's main army into a retreat through the maze of twisting, swampy roads where it could be annihilated, too.

Jackson was to slip down from the valley on the side of the river occupied by the McClellan men under General Fitz-John Porter. Following his attack on Porter's right flank, other Confederate divisions under Generals Ambrose Powell Hill, Daniel Harvey Hill and James Longstreet were to force the bridges and hit Porter on the front and left. Everything depended upon boldness and timing.

The whole plan relied on Jackson. Those in on the secret of his coming counted upon him as on a legendary hero. He was the South's marvel and the Union's dread. Lee's strategy was shaped around Stonewall's swift, hard-hitting powers. The other generals could not safely move until he was in the rear of Porter, for otherwise they would run head-on in frontal attack on an entrenched Union army. Longstreet, who had once referred to Jackson and his men as "the second-raters in the valley," asked Stonewall when he could strike.

Promptly Jackson said he would be on hand the next day, June 24, ready for battle on the 25th. Doubtful, Longstreet urged that Jackson give himself more time. Finally, it was agreed that Stonewall would attack early in the morning of the 26th. Then he rode back to his army, which was now at Beaver Dam Station, fifteen miles northwest of Richmond. They had marched there badly, lacking his personal command. On the 25th, still tired, they seemed languid in the flat, hot, dusty country so different from the valley. And Jackson did not seem able to press them. The crucial hour came at dawn on the 26th. Jackson was not there.

Many excuses have been offered since. The country through which he came was such a tangle that local guides got lost. They were misled by new roads which McClellan's men had cut through thickets which one of them said "an old hare could not get through." Probably the most important fact was that "Old Jack" was not made of iron. He had had only ten hours' sleep during the four days before the battle. Whatever the cause, his absence contributed to a bloody repulse of the Confederates fighting through swamps against the un-flanked and fortified Union troops. The Rebels had hit the Union men hard, nevertheless, and word had reached the Yankees, too, that Jackson was coming—at last.

Next day Jackson fought at Gaines' Mill and, though late again, this time with all his old fire. He had been lost once more on the twisting roads through the woods. He had hung back near Old Cold Harbor in strict con-formance with what he believed to be General Lee's orders. Then late in the afternoon, as the Confederates seemed to be getting the worst of it, Jackson sucked hard at his lemon, listening to the increasing roar of the battle being fought by Ambrose Hill and Longstreet. There was no time to be lost. After dark Porter could slip across the Chickahominy, burn his bridges and join McClellan in the movement of his base south from the Pamunkey River to the James. At such a time, a hot and dusty Jackson met Lee who seemed always immaculate even on the battlefield.

"Ah, General," said Lee, "I'm very glad to see you."

"Ah, General," said Lee, "I am very glad to see you. I had hoped to be with you before."

It was a gentle rebuke for tardiness. Jackson must take his men in quickly. And he did. With only an hour of daylight left, his men poured in. A half hour went by. In the thickest of the fighting Jackson's voice rose "with the deadly clang of a rifle."

"This affair must hang in suspense no longer," he shouted. "Sweep the field with the bayonet."

From the right side of his line the listening Lee suddenly heard the Rebel Yell. The Yankee line broke and scattered toward the Chickahominy. It was a great victory. Richmond rejoiced hilariously when Lee's news came. But 8,000 Rebels were dead, wounded or missing. Too many of Porter's men got away.

Then Jackson fell into the doldrums again. As Lee pressed McClellan, joined by Porter's battered corps in his retreat, the Confederate leader thought he had the Yankees in a trap on June 30 beyond White Oak Swamp. There Jackson failed to bring his men into the battle again. His force, the largest in Lee's army, had crossed the Chickahominy and reached the White Oak

Bridge at midday. Stonewall halted there to reconnoiter the crossing of White Oak Creek.

Then he seemed to go into a sort of stupor. The creek was not deep; its bottom was firm. Officers found other crossings. The wide swamp of dark waters spreading among hardwoods and vines was a serious obstacle but not such as would ordinarily have held Stonewall in check. Jackson lagged. Not far on the other side of the stream Longstreet and A. P. Hill came into furious encounter with McClellan's great though retreating force. They needed only Jackson in the Union rear to beat and bottle up the Yankee army. But Jackson stayed where he was on the hot, steamy edge of the swamp.

During the crucial hours he seemed half asleep. Though the fighting Confederates once broke the Federal lines, with Jackson's men they might have destroyed the army. Instead McClellan's troops got away to a low bluff which rose in the swampy country near the bank of the James. Malvern Hill would be long remembered as the sloping ground upon which row after row of charging Confederates fell before blazing ranks of Union artillery. Night fell on horror there. One of

Jackson's men recalled passing over ground where D. H. Hill's North Carolina troops had fought and hearing the many wounded scream and then call out in last hope the names of their regiments. Many North Carolina boys were lost forever there in the bloody dark.

Next morning, as Jackson told his doubting fellow officers would be the case, the Union forces did not attack. They had fallen back. The Confederates did not follow.

The terrible Seven Days were over. The South hailed another Confederate victory in the delivery of Richmond. McClellan had been driven back though at the greatest cost—and a cost which the Confederacy increasingly could not afford. But Lee's plan had been the destruction of the Union army. It had failed. And ever since critics have been debating Stonewall Jackson's part in the failure.

Stonewall never admitted any. The only line of excuse he ever wrote was perhaps one in a letter to his wife in which he said he had "not been well, have suffered from fever and debility, but through the blessing

of an ever-kind Providence I am much better today."
Obviously he was an exhausted man who had presumed
beyond the physical powers with which Providence had
endowed him. Sometimes he seemed mentally as well as
physically lost in the strange country of thickets, dust,
steam and heat. His old Lexington friend, General
Daniel Hill, in a somewhat backhanded defense of him,
said that "the hooded falcon cannot strike the quarry."
By this he meant that Jackson could fight only when
independent of superiors. Lee knew better than that.
Jackson was to show it.

Obviously, however, Stonewall was in no mood of
triumph. He did not seem blessed by Providence. His
staff remembered the end of the Seven Days in terms of
their chief's towering rage. His bristling fury had
grown all day on July 3rd. When a guide came in that
evening with a fumbling report of roads and directions,
Jackson ordered him from his presence with threats of
extreme punishment. In cold anger as he went to bed
he told his staff that his Negro servant, Jim, would have
breakfast for them "punctually at dawn."

"I expect you to be up, to eat immediately and be in

the saddle with me. We must burn no more daylight."

Only one of his staff, Major Dabney, was up when Jackson came down in the dawn.

"Major, how is it this staff will never be punctual?"

"I am on time," the clergyman-soldier replied. "I cannot control the others."

Stonewall turned on the servant. "Jim, put that food into the chest, lock it, have the chest in the wagon and that wagon moving in two minutes. Do you hear?"

Too angry to eat, Jackson rode off. Jim stared after him.

"My stars," said Jim to the Major, "but the Gen'rul is jus' mad this time. Mos' like lightnin' strike him."

Jackson's lightning would never be late again.

10

Three Cigars

By this time ragged Rebels in Virginia no longer had any false ideas about the bravery of Yankee soldiers. The notion that one Reb could beat ten Yanks had been revised in bloody action, particularly when courageous Northern soldiers had better guns and magnificent equipment. Yet, confident that they were better led, the morale of the Confederate soldiers was excellent. In the lengthening summer of 1862, Southern hopes were at high tide.

Still, Lee and Jackson knew that no defensive strategy would do against growing Union forces. The North had the most money and the most men; its industries could equip new and bigger armies. To win, the South had to hit before that was done. Lee's purpose then was not to defend Richmond but to drive the Yankees out of Virginia. It was time for an offensive. McClellan, who had recently seemed about to march into Richmond, now lay behind entrenchments which he had thrown up against Lee under the cover of Federal gunboats. So while Lee waited to see what McClellan might do, he sent Jackson westward to Gordonsville. There the enemy Old Jack faced was not the cautious McClellan but a newcomer to the Virginia front, General John Pope. He might fight better, certainly he talked louder. He told his own men that "I come to you from the West where we have always seen the backs of our enemies."

Pope told his soldiers to stop talking about "lines of retreat and bases of supply." Instead, he said, "Let us study the probable lines of retreat of our enemies, and leave our own to take care of themselves." As for himself, he said, he would have his "headquarters in the saddle." That remark led later to jokes that Pope "had his headquarters where his hind quarters ought to be." Boastful as he was, Pope was no laughing matter to the Confederates.

Lincoln had put together under Pope in an Army of Virginia all the old forces of Frémont, Banks and Mc-Dowell which Jackson had defeated one by one in the valley. In one body they were big and dangerous. Furthermore, Pope demanded and was promised more men from McClellan's army which had been pushed down the rivers in the Seven Days. Pope's army, poised between the Rappahannock and the Rapidan rivers west of Fredericksburg, was increasing in size. Time, as always, was on the side of the Yankees.

Lee left the first blow to Jackson's "reflection and good judgment." His faith in Stonewall had not decreased but grown. The Virginia patrician and the mountain man had come to that Southern partnership in which Jackson said he would follow Lee blindfolded and Lee regarded Old Jack as his dependable first lieutenant. Stonewall took a first hard swipe at part of Pope's army on August 9, at Cedar Mountain, seven miles south of Culpeper Court House. There he hit a division under a familiar foe, General "Commissary"

Banks, who, Old Jack said, "is always ready to fight . . . and . . . generally gets whipped."

That was not so certain this time. Though Jackson had Banks outnumbered, the Massachusetts politician-soldier gave Old Jack rough opposition. Once he broke the left flank of Jackson's line. Jackson's superior forces drove him back, however, with heavy loss. At his old game Jackson had mauled a segment of a greater force, but he drew back across the Rapidan as Pope's whole army came up. He waited there for Lee and did not have to wait long. As McClellan's men left the James River for Washington, Lee moved all but a few of his forces from Richmond. Joining Jackson along the Rapidan, he had a Confederate army of 55,000 men. Across the stream Pope had 70,000 men with the prospect of 50,000 more from McClellan's army.

In the warm sun in a little village called Jefferson on August 24, 1862, Lee and Jackson talked together a long time. Their soldiers at a respectful distance watched Lee listening while Stonewall talked. Old Jack jerked his head. He raised his left arm with the palm turned outward in a familiar gesture. With the toe of his big boot he drew maps in the dust. Lee nodded gravely. Probably they talked of a plan Jackson had been urging since the first Battle of Manassas for an invasion of the North. Certainly at about that time Lee reached the decision to divide his army in the face of a greater force. It was a bold and risky enterprise. Division of their forces by the Yankees had, as Stonewall put it, helped Providence bless his arms in the Valley campaign. All the same, Lee's decision set the Rebel forces in motion on an almost unequaled thirty-day campaign. It was marked with courage, boldness and both good luck and bad.

The first bad luck had already occurred when Lee and Jackson talked at Jefferson. The redoubtable Confederate cavalry leader, J. E. B. Stuart, who wore a peacock's plume in his hat and had his gray coat lined with red, was responsible for that. Surprised, Stuart was almost captured, lost his plumed hat and, more important, a leather haversack containing information about Lee's first plan to attack Pope's army along the Rappahannock. Then, turnabout, Stuart in a raid on Pope's headquarters brought off that boastful General's dispatch book. It gave warning of the arrival of Union reinforcements from McClellan and that time was short if the Confederates hoped to beat Pope. The third item of luck, coming later, would involve Confederate secrets written on a paper wrapped around three cigars. That paper may have saved the Union.

When Lee reached his decision in the talk at Jefferson, the incident of the cigars was an unforeseen item of the future. Now Stonewall was moving the next morning. No tardiness attended the start of his men in the dawn of August 25th. On his little horse Jackson led his men westward, leaving Lee and Longstreet with only half the Confederate force before Pope's big army. Stonewall's "foot cavalry," as it was called because it sometimes outmarched mounted men, swung out at a rapid pace. It was not necessary for Jackson to repeat, "Press on, men, close up." They crossed the Rappahannock high upstream. Of course, with Jackson leading they did not know where they were going. Some thought they were on their way back to the Valley, to Winchester, to Harpers Ferry.

The Rappahannock was left behind. The Bull Run Mountains were to the east. Guessing their destination only by landmarks, the men were in fine fettle. As the General rode along the line not grumbles but cheers greeted him. He tried to stop them: "Don't shout, boys,

With the toe of his big boot he drew maps in the dust

the Yankees will hear you." They marched till mid-
night, hit the road again at dawn with little more
breakfast than raw corn and fruit they picked by the
roadsides. Then suddenly as they turned through Thor-
oughfare Gap in the Bull Run Mountains, the men
knew they were marching to the rear of Pope's army.

This was the greatest march of Jackson's brief career.
His 20,000 men covered fifty-one miles in two days.
Of this mission, one of the ablest foreign students of his
campaigns said, "neither strategically nor tactically did

[he] make a single mistake." The South as well as his soldiers then shared the feeling of his invincibility. In his worn cap on ugly Little Sorrel, his men adored him even when they could not understand him. Bald-headed, hard-fighting General Ewell said that he "never saw one of Jackson's couriers approach without expecting an order to assault the North Pole." All counted on his success. Excitement spread in the ranks of the marching men as the knowledge spread on the downgrade from Bull Run Mountain that they were moving to Manassas where Old Jack and his brigade just thirteen months before had won their Stonewall name.

Stonewall seemed to be pausing for a special celebration. Throwing his main body across Pope's path, he led his men, not to battle, but to Pope's base of supply about which that General had spoken so scornfully. The ragged Rebels regarded the supplies with awe. There was a little fighting there. Stuart's horsemen had attended to that. The "foot cavalry" gave its attention to the rows of warehouses overflowing with all the things those ragamuffin marchers lacked. First, Jackson put guards on a warehouse of whisky and put trusted men to pouring it out. ("I fear it more than Pope.") Then he let his men gorge themselves on the abundance of food and clothing.

They found strange little fishes in tins, fancy underwear, molasses and shoes. There were mountains of matériel—arms, guns, ammunition. It was multiplied Christmas for every man. Each took the things he wanted most. Some specialized in shoes and hung extra pairs about their necks. Others filled their canteens with molasses. All ate till they were bloated. Jackson let them satisfy themselves to the full. Then, with his army refurnished and overfed and with as much of the supplies as he could pack into captured wagons, the great depot was set on fire. Stonewall's men moved out in the light of the blaze. The fire was a torch to carry the news to Pope.

That General thought that only cavalry raiders were behind him until he saw the great volcano of fire and smoke which rose where his supplies had been. Turning, he set out to "bag the whole crowd" including the great prize of the famous Stonewall himself. Pope was sure he would catch him when Jackson showed where he was by attacking one of Pope's divisions as it marched on the Warrenton Turnpike. This time Jackson was

Each man took the things he wanted most

not just attacking a body of isolated troops. He baited
Pope to come after him out of a strong entrenched position. Pope came headlong, but with his divisions scattered, to catch his prize. The Confederates would have
had less chance against him if he had stayed in his entrenched position. Instead he moved to fight on the
ground Jackson had chosen, and where he waited for
Longstreet to join him.

Jackson took a long risk in bringing down upon his men Pope's whole army. But at Groveton, six miles northwest of Manassas, he occupied the strongest ground behind an unfinished railroad cut and an embankment. Pope attacked with his badly scattered forces. His men fought bravely but at the end of the day the Union General had wrecked half his army in five assaults though he still had 30,000 fresh men. Jackson's men had been badly battered. This time Longstreet was late in joining the fighting. Pope attacked again in confidence that Jackson had fallen back. He met instead Jackson's hidden men, then at last the army of Longstreet. Longstreet's flanking artillery cut the Union soldiers down like the swing of a scythe. In a great counterstroke Lee sent his whole force to sweep Pope's army from the field.

Behind the fortifications of Washington, another great Union army now was demoralized in defeat. Yet 9,000 Confederates had fallen at Manassas. The work of the weary Rebels was not done. Lee let the army rest one day. Then he began the movement Jackson had long urged. Lee's reunited army, still smelling of battle, crossed the Potomac into Maryland. None of them realized then that their fate there might be in a paper wrapped around three cigars.

The lean, tattered, sometimes shoeless army marched into Maryland singing a new song about "the despot's heel is on thy shore, Maryland, my Maryland." No such turnout of new recruits appeared as the Confederates had hoped. Ladies seemed more enthusiastic than men of military age. Many people were friendly and brought delicacies to the hungry soldiers. Others showed strong Union feeling. When Jackson went to church in Frederick the preacher prayed for President Lincoln. Old Jack, however, missed the defiance as he had fallen asleep at the services as he often did. The story made popular by the poet, John Greenleaf Whittier, about an old lady named Barbara Frietchie defying Jackson to shoot down her American flag, never happened. Perhaps the most friendly attitude was that expressed by another old lady who, with tears in her eyes, during that campaign cried, "God bless your dirty, ragged souls!"

Yankee garrisons in the area did not retreat, however, as Lee had expected. His supply line to Virginia was threatened by Union posts on the Potomac. So once again Lee in enemy territory decided to divide his army. Reluctantly Jackson, who was not sure it was a good idea this time, set out with 23,000 men on the morning of September 10, to clean out the Union strongholds between Lee's army and Virginia.

It was a triumphal march. Along the Potomac Jackson found that all the Union posts had concentrated at Harpers Ferry. He was attacked by adoring ladies who wanted to hug and kiss him, to get a button from his coat. But when they began to ask for locks of his hair, he retreated. He was less afraid of the Yankees in Harpers Ferry. At the beginning of the war he had seen how hard that town might be to defend. Now he occupied the heights around it, and trained his guns upon it. Only limited fighting was necessary then. The garrison of 12,000 Union soldiers surrendered. Some of the Yankees seemed proud to have been captured by Stonewall Jackson.

"Boys," said one, "he's not much for looks, but if we had him we wouldn't have got caught in this trap."

Without knowing it, Jackson and the rest of Lee's army were in a greater trap then. When Lee decided to

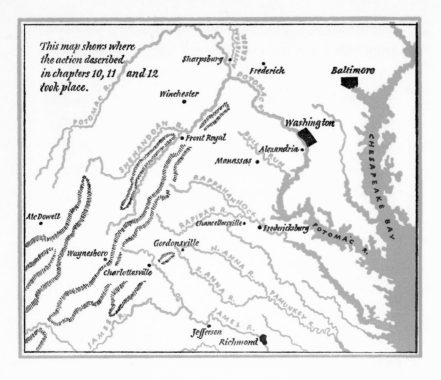

This map shows where the action described in chapters 10, 11 and 12 took place.

divide his army in Maryland he had embodied his plans in "Confidential Special Order No. 191." Longstreet chewed his copy up and swallowed it. Jackson memorized and destroyed his copy. As he departed on his mission on September 10, he had acted to mystify everybody including his own men as to where he was going. But on September 13, when Jackson surrounded Harpers Ferry, General McClellan, who had been given another chance after Pope's defeat, came into Frederick from which Lee had moved westward. Also on that day a young Yankee private, B. W. Mitchell, Company F, 27th Indiana, stooped and picked up three cigars wrapped in a paper. The paper was Lee's Order No. 191. Swept quickly up the ranks from private to sergeant to staff, the paper told the overcautious McClellan that Lee's limited forces were scattered.

McClellan wrote to President Lincoln, "Here is a paper with which, if I cannot whip Bobby Lee I will be willing to go home."

And Lincoln replied soberly, "Destroy the Rebel army if possible."

There seemed a good chance that he would. Greatly outnumbered as McClellan approached, Lee was sending desperate word to the commanders of his divided army. Jackson's "foot cavalry" was on the road, given little time to enjoy the supplies they had captured at Harpers Ferry. On the way to Sharpsburg where Lee waited, Old Jack pressed his men on all night long on a march which even he later described as "severe."

11

Old Jack or a Rabbit

Stonewall did not reach the village of Sharpsburg beside Antietam Creek any too soon. Indeed, if McClellan had not grown cautious again despite his possession of Lee's Order 191, the battle might have begun the same early morn he arrived. A surprisingly belligerent McClellan had hit some of Lee's army hard at South Mountain but brave resistance gave Lee more time. Waiting for his absent troops, he determined to fight though some of his officers counseled retreat. Jackson found Lee optimistic though he had seen with his field glasses the approach of the great blue Union host of 80,000 men. Stonewall approved Lee's decision to fight.

McClellan's old caution gave the Confederates another day. More of Jackson's men arrived. And on the night of September 16, 1862, they waited on the left of Lee's line in a meadow between two wooded stretches along the creek. Those woods, the meadow, cornfields, a contested road called Bloody Lane, were soon to be filled with the bodies of young men in blue and gray in the single bloodiest day of the war.

Across Antietam Creek which flowed into the nearby Potomac, the Federal horde was poised. It came running out of the dawn to hit Jackson's men hard on the left of Lee's line. General "Fighting Joe" Hooker, whom Jackson was to meet again at Chancellorsville, led the first wave of the Federal assault. Behind bushes, stone fences and limestone ledges the Rebs waited for the blow and met it. Pushed back inch by inch by the larger forces, the Southerners fought hand to hand, held ground, threatened counterattack. But before any strike back could be launched, a new fresh body of Federals was thrown against the Confederates who fought, as they so often did, without reserves.

A wide gap was cut in the Southern lines, but the exhausted Yankees who made it were unable to press on. They were glad to hold the gain they had made. That seemed enough with a third Union force of 18,000 more fresh men forming behind them. Fortunately then Lee, moving his limited forces back and forth to the points under fiercest assault along his thin line, moved men to Jackson. Old Jack was not thinking only of more desperate resistance; his mind turned naturally to attack. Earlier he had been angry when a North Carolina regiment fell back fast after an attack on Federal guns. He scoffed at its commander's report of the force before him and sent a volunteer private up a tree to report on the numbers.

"How many troops can you see over there?"

The young soldier shouted down, "Oceans of them."

"Count the flags, sir," Jackson barked.

"One, two, three——" He counted faster as sharpshooters snipped the leaves about him, but he continued till he reached "Thirty-nine."

Even for Stonewall that was too many for a charge with his remaining men. He waited. He seemed undisturbed nevertheless. He sucked his lemon, thinking. Before him riderless horses screamed and reared where their riders had fallen. The field was thick with the bodies of boys. Some Confederate stragglers were rushing back in panic. The new Federal force was coming up. Then, despite the surging blue ocean coming on, Jackson sent the remnants of his men and the divisions sent to help him in a countercharge against the confident Yankees. Rushing forward shouting the Rebel Yell, they cut down the Union soldiers like corn.

"God has been good to us this day," Stonewall said. But Providence had provided no victory. The Confederate charge was halted and men on both sides, standing deep among the bodies of the dead, slowed and rested where they stood. It was at that point that young Dr. McGuire, Jackson's surgeon, appalled by the casualties, came up to suggest the removal of the Confederate hospital across the Potomac. The doctor had some peaches. Jackson munched one.

"Doctor McGuire," he said, "they have done their worst."

That was true of the fighting before Jackson. But McClellan struck elsewhere along the line. Much of his failure to break it was due to the piecemeal manner in which he threw in his magnificent army. Once later in the day Jackson had hoped to turn the enemy's right wing and attack him in the rear. "We'll drive McClellan into the Potomac," he said. Unfortunately, he found that Federal wing securely posted upon the Potomac, guarded by more and better guns than the Confederates could throw against them. It was remarkable that Jackson even contemplated such audacity in so desperate a situation. Still, the day ended with a triumphant sound for the Confederates when the Rebel Yell, as darkness came on, announced the repulse of the Union General Ambrose E. Burnside. That bewhiskered general was not able to hold the bridge at the other end of the line which he had forced across Antietam Creek.

The darkness was welcome. Jackson had fought with only 19,000 troops and had beaten off thirty thousand. The enemy had had one hundred cannon to his forty. Lee said that he had less than 40,000 men in the battle. McClellan had 80,000, though more than 20,000 never got into action. Against Lee's tired, torn army, they were still available, however. The darkness came down on the dead, the dying and those living who might have to fight again in the morning.

Jackson joined the other generals in Lee's field headquarters. Each had reports of his own losses among the 10,000 Confederates lying dead or dying that night. Some officers suggested immediate retreat in the dark. Lee made his decision. He could not launch an offensive next day, but if Little Mac wanted a fight in the morning the Confederates would be there to give it to him. Satisfied with the decision, Old Jack went back to his camp in an open field near town among the blinking lanterns of litter bearers still seeking the wounded in the dark.

McClellan did not attack in the morning, though reinforcements greater than his losses had been brought up. Then Lee, who had no reinforcements, considered a final effort to hit and turn the Federal right wing. He sent Jackson forward to scout the situation. The line bristled with rifled cannon. The Southerners had only short-range, smooth-bore guns to use against them. Stonewall consulted with his artillerists. Then he came reluctantly back to Lee to report that such an attempt

They rushed forward in a countercharge, shouting the

Rebel Yell, **and** *cut down the Union soldiers like corn*

would be suicidal. Sadly he joined in the view that the prudent course would be retreat back to Virginia. But he added that though Providence had not provided a victory at Sharpsburg it "was better to have fought in Maryland than to have left it without a struggle."

Many were left behind never to return. The dead still covered the field. There were stragglers who had slipped away from the fighting. Others were prisoners in Union hands. It was a grim silent day. But at least one story comes down of a Rebel prisoner who kept his saucy defiance even in Federal hands. Herded to the Federal rear, he stopped to admire an array of artillery with each barrel marked "U.S."

"I swear, Mister," he said to his captors, "you all has got almost as many of these-here U.S. guns as we'uns has."

Little humor marked the retreat across the Potomac which Lee began at dark. Jackson watched scowling as the guns, wagons and men poured across Boteler's Ford on the Potomac. One of Jackson's old V.M.I. cadets, James H. Lane, with his North Carolina troops, was entrusted with the command of the rear guard in the passage of the Potomac. Lee said, "Thank God," when the last of his army crossed the ford. All was not over, however. Suddenly after the army had camped a few miles back from the river, Federals pushed over the Potomac and seized the cannon put there to prevent their crossing. Old Jack sent forces to push them back into the river.

"With the blessing of God," said Stonewall, "they will soon be driven back."

He rode forward to watch it and noted, as his men shot by the score the bluecoats floundering in the stream, that it was "an appalling scene of destruction of human life." Invasion was over. Pursuit had been repulsed. Across the river the battered Confederate Army rested. They needed it. Time was required to refit the dirty, ragged men, to heal the wounded, to round up with no gentleness the too many stragglers and deserters.

Yet, Old Jack seemed to relax. Once, at the hospitable house of a Virginian, he asked for a little white sugar when a big bottle of whisky was passed around and said, "Come, gentlemen, let's take a drink."

That was a rare thing with him. This was almost the only drink his staff had ever seen him take by choice. And on this occasion he admitted that he liked the taste too much so that he seldom ever touched it. He seemed in a strangely expansive mood after the failure of the invasion. His old V.M.I. student, Jim Lane, the thirty-year-old General who had commanded the rear guard in the Potomac crossing, visited Jackson's quarters then for the first time.

"I wondered if he would recognize me," Lane recalled later. "I certainly expected to receive his orders in a few terse sentences . . . He knew me as soon as I entered his tent, though we had not met for years. He rose quickly, with a smile on his face, took my hand in both of his in the warmest manner . . . familiarly calling me Lane, whereas it had always been Mr. Lane at the Institute . . . Then, for the first time, I began to love that reserved man."

Neither Jackson nor Lane dreamed then that Old Jack and Lane's quick-triggered North Carolinians would have a tragic rendezvous seven months later in April at Chancellorsville. Lane was not the only one who realized that his affection for Stonewall was growing. Southerners showered him with gifts, food, furniture, horses. But Old Jack lived much as his men did. If many of them were ragged, there was no spit-and-

Old Jack lived much as his men did

polish quality about their commander, either. He wore a dirty uniform and a soft hat with which he had replaced his famous old cap. He maintained no elaborate headquarters. Often his eccentricities were exaggerated by his men who liked to think of him as an odd military genius. Serving with Jackson was no easy business. He drove, marched, pressed, fought his men. They griped and complained, loved him and fought for him. He gave them victory and a pride often lit by humor.

"I wish all Yankees were in hell," said a tired, lean man in the Stonewall Brigade.

"I don't," said another, "because Old Jack would have us standing picket at the gate before night and in there before morning—and it's too hot where we is to suit me."

Old Jack drilled them hard, building their morale again, in that autumn interlude between battles. Lee was reorganizing a more efficient army, too. On October 11, he made Jackson one of the two lieutenant-generals just authorized by the Confederate Congress. And he added, looking back to the Maryland invasion behind them: "My opinion of the merits of General Jackson has been greatly enhanced during this expedition. He is true, honest and brave; has a single eye to the good of the service, and spares no exertion to accomplish his object."

Jackson's promotion seemed natural and proper to his men. They were proud of him, but they had a special sense of their distinction as his soldiers before the promotion. With his new eminence, they did not lose the humor which they always added to their affection for him. When a jubilant shouting sounded down the line in their camps, they grinned and cried to each other, "Boys, look out! Here's Old Jack or a rabbit!"

They laughed because they loved him.

12

Gold Lace for Stonewall

When Stonewall's uniform seemed most stained and worn, General J. E. B. Stuart, the gay cavalryman, sent him a present. It was a fine gray uniform-coat elegantly decorated with "gilt buttons and sheeny facings and gold lace." Old Jack blushed at the idea of such magnificence. Reluctantly he put it on. When he wore it to dinner his staff was amazed. Old Jim, his servant, almost dropped the dishes. The rumor of the change in the General's appearance ran swiftly through the camps of his ragged men. They were delighted. Soldiers, one officer recalled, "came running by hundreds to the spot, desirous of seeing their beloved Stonewall in his new attire."

"God A'mighty," one hilarious Reb yelled, "Old Jack has drawed his bounty money and got hiss'f some clo'se."

The affection and respect in which Stonewall was held was never more evident than in that golden autumn. Jackson made his headquarters at Winchester in the valley which regarded him as its own. Visitors came to see him there from all parts of the South, and even from England where his military exploits had won mounting admiration. All sorts of presents came to him. Newspapers in the South were filled with his story. So were those in the North though he was sometimes magnified as monster there—but a monster entitled to great respect. A ballad about him, "Stonewall Jackson's Way" (written by John W. Palmer, a newspaper correspondent, within the sound of the fighting at Antietam), spread from the camps to the whole South:

Come, stack arms, men! Pile on the rails,
  Stir up the camp-fire bright;
No matter if the canteen fails,
  We'll make a roaring night.
Here Shenandoah brawls along,
There burley Blue Ridge echoes strong,
To swell the brigade's rousing song
  Of "Stonewall Jackson's Way."

We see him now—the old slouched hat
  Cocked o'er his eye askew;
The shrewd, dry smile; the speech so pat,
  So calm, so blunt, so true.
The "Blue-Light Elder" knows 'em well:
Says he, "That's Banks—he's fond of shell;
Lord save his soul! we'll give him—" well,
  That's "Stonewall Jackson's Way."

Silence! ground arms! kneel all! caps off!
  Old Blue-Light's going to pray.
Strangle the fool that dares to scoff!
  Attention! it's his way.
Appealing from his native sod,
In *forma pauperis* to God—
"Lay bare thine arm, stretch forth thy rod!
  Amen!" That's "Stonewall's Way."

He's in the saddle now. Fall in!
  Steady, the whole brigade!
Hill's at the ford, cut off—we'll win
  His way out, ball and blade!
What matter if our shoes are worn?
What matter if our feet are torn?
"Quick-step! we're with him before dawn!"
  That's "Stonewall Jackson's Way."

The sun's bright lances rout the mists
  Of morning, and, by George,
Here's Longstreet struggling in the lists,
  Hemmed in an ugly gorge.
Pope and his Yankees, whipped before,
"Bay'nets and grape!" hear Stonewall roar;
"Charge, Stuart! Pay off Ashby's score!"
  Is "Stonewall Jackson's Way."

Ah, maiden, wait and watch and yearn
  For news of Stonewall's band!
Ah, widow, read with eyes that burn
  That ring upon thy hand.
Ah, wife, sew on, pray on, hope on!
Thy life shall not be all forlorn.
The foe had better ne'er been born
  That gets in "Stonewall's Way."

The ragged, singing men also made up fables about him. In the Bible story, they said, Moses took forty years bringing the Israelites through the wilderness. Old Jack would have taken them through at the double-quick on half rations in three days. There was also the earthy parable: "Stonewall died, and two angels came down from Heaven to take him back with them. They went to his tent; he was not there. They went to the hospital; he was not there. They went to the prayer meeting; he was not there. They had to return without him. But when they reported he had disappeared, they found that he had made a flank march and reached Heaven before them."

Such singing, storytelling days did not last. On November 22, 1862, his Second Corps of the Army of Northern Virginia marched from Winchester with Stonewall leading his men out of his beloved valley for the last time. Lee had called him eastward where, at Fredericksburg along the Rappahannock River, a larger Union army than any ever formed before was approaching on a new direct march on Richmond. On the heights south of the river which the forces of the new Union commander, General Ambrose E.

Burnside, had to bridge to cross, Lee had drawn up his troops to receive the attack. Also, unknown to Burnside, Jackson's corps had come up to hide in the woods along the river shore. Snow covered the ground. Ragged men shivered in the cold. But they waited to massacre the great plumed army of men in blue.

Burnside had his pontoon bridges across the river. He sent in a magnificent force of men. Once they broke through Jackson's lines in a little swampy stretch of woods. Stonewall ordered the bayonet. They were driven out. Artillery from above tore into the massed Federal lines. Finally a charge of Jackson's men screeching the Rebel Yell almost drove the Federals into the river, being stopped only by big Federal guns on the other shore. But the river bank became a slaughter pen. Federal soldiers had shown themselves as dogged and brave as the Confederates, but at Fredericksburg more than twice as many Yanks as Rebs were killed and wounded. Their bodies covered the field and when night came mercifully to stop the fighting, the ragged, cold Confederates slipped out in the darkness to strip the bodies of blankets and clothes.

Jackson had wanted to fight on in the dark. Young

Dr. McGuire, once more all but overwhelmed by the bloody task of dealing with the wounded, told about that later.

"After Burnside's repulse," he said, "Jackson asked me how many bandages I had. I told him, and asked why he wanted to know. He said that he wanted to have a piece of white cloth to tie on each man's arm so that his soldiers might recognize each other in a night attack, and he asked to be allowed to make such an attack, and drive his foe into the river or capture him. Subsequent events demonstrated that he knew the state of things within the hostile lines, and would have accomplished his purpose."

Such an attack was not undertaken. Next morning one of Stonewall's aides reported that he was "walking about his tent like a caged lion. The Yankee music across the Rappahannock greatly annoys him." Later that day a heavy storm permitted the Union forces to recross the stream. The Confederates waited hopefully for Burnside to resume the attack. Two days passed. Then on the morning of the third the great Union army was gone. The Confederacy had won again but Lee and Jackson knew that the Union had retired to prepare a still greater force against the more and more ragged, limited, hungry forces of the South.

Southern politicians were elated. President Davis talked as if the war would soon be over. He thought the North would give up. He still expected England to recognize the Confederacy. Jackson and Lee understood that all they had won was a respite. Even that, like the interlude in the autumn before, was welcome. Stonewall took up his headquarters in the one-room hunting lodge of a plantation at Moss Neck, eleven miles south of Fredericksburg. And there on Christmas, less than two weeks after the battle, Lee, Longstreet, and Stuart came for dinner with Jackson and his staff.

Between battles, in the midst of a more and more destitute South, it was a warmly lit occasion. Admirers had sent a great turkey and oysters; one lady sent a rare pad of fine butter with the image of a fighting cock stamped upon it. The gay Stuart took his cue from the cock on the butter and the prints of race horses and fighting cocks on the walls of the hunting lodge to tease the serious Stonewall. The fine food, he said, the rooster on the butter, the sporting prints on the wall, all obviously indicated the true tastes of General Jackson. While the guests in their best uniforms laughed, Stuart shook his head: he feared that Stonewall's moral character was in process of rapid decline. Jackson grinned in response to the laughter. He even hinted slyly, remembering times on his Uncle Cummins' place, that he might know more about race horses and fighting cocks than General Stuart suggested in all his banter. All that seemed long, long ago though Jackson on that last, briefly gay Christmas was only thirty-eight years old.

Drilling went on. Bodies of troops were sent off to forage for food for men and horses. Also, Stonewall encouraged the religious activities which had always been dear to his heart. In this winter and spring a wave of evangelical zeal swept the army. The soldiers built a log church for services which Stonewall regularly attended. No solemnity marked his faith, however. He had time for playfulness as well as prayer. Two little girls in the neighborhood captured him and he so capitulated as to let them cut off locks of his hair.

Lee, Longstreet, and Stuart joined him for Christmas

"Well, you may have a little," he told them, "if you promise not to take any gray hairs."

"Oh, General Jackson," the girls said, laughing, "you are a young man, you have no gray hairs."

Stonewall smiled. "Why, don't you know the soldiers call me Old Jack?"

It seemed a sort of young time. And on April 20,

1863, Anna Jackson came on the crowded cars from Richmond with their baby daughter, Julia, just five months old. She had been born while Jackson was crossing the Massanutten from the valley on the way to Fredericksburg. The reunion with Anna marked a special happy and contented time. The baby was baptized. General Lee came to call. "There is," an officer wrote, "much importance pertaining to the 'Lieutenant Generaless.'"

April was beautiful in Virginia but that meant that the winter-bogged roads were drying. Armies would be moving. On April 29, nine days after Anna and the baby came, an adjutant woke Stonewall early in the morning. Across the Rappahannock the Union General, "Fighting Joe" Hooker, showed signs of new restlessness. The adjutant brought Stonewall news of Yankee movement.

"That looks as if Hooker were crossing," Jackson said. He swung out of bed. The time had come to send Anna back to safety. He kissed her, hugged the baby, then rode off toward the front without breakfast. Hooker had moved. And Longstreet with his corps was off in North Carolina on a food-gathering

The time had come to send Anna back to safety

mission. But Lee and Jackson were alert. The Confederate army's morale was high even though its shoes were broken and its rations thin. Its faith in its leaders was never higher. General George Pickett, who later was to lead at Gettysburg the courageous charge to the South's last high hope, wrote his wife about Stonewall.

"I only pray that God may spare him to us to see us through. If General Lee had Grant's resources he

★ 161 ☆

would soon end the war; but Old Jack can do it without resources."

On that spring morning of April 29, Stonewall rode straight to the smoke and the sound of cannon booming along the Rappahannock Valley. The Battle of Chancellorsville had begun.

13

The Fallen Sword

Along the Rappahannock, Hooker's guns boomed in increasing belligerence. There were conflicting reports as to what that new Union leader with his vast army of 130,000 men planned to do. Word came to the Confederates that large bodies of his men were moving up the river. Evidently he planned no such frontal attack on the 62,500 Rebs before him as Burnside had tried to his disaster in December. Then it became clear that Hooker's main force had crossed the river upstream beyond the Southern fortifications. He was preparing to move through the tangled woods called the Wilderness, force Lee's retreat and attack him in open country. With men to spare he had left another large army facing Lee at Fredericksburg. Now he announced to his army, "Our enemy must either ingloriously fly or come out from behind his defenses, and give us battle on our own ground, where certain destruction awaits him."

Lee and Jackson were not contemplating their destruction. Jackson was for attacking the troops across the river which Hooker had left on their front. Then, after observing the tremendous artillery of the enemy, he changed his mind. Instead he agreed that the thing to do was to attack Hooker's main army before it got through the Wilderness. This meant once again dividing the army. Jackson moved hard, fought hard, and met stronger Union forces than mere skirmishers. Contact seemed to be growing into a battle. Then suddenly on the early afternoon of May 1, the Federals withdrew into the forest, giving Jackson such an easy victory that he was suspicious.

Stonewall galloped to the front with General Stuart. Suddenly they were under heavy artillery fire. Masked batteries hit men and horses all around them. Jackson was undisturbed. He seemed invulnerable in the hottest fire. He had seen enough to show him that Hooker, faced with the unexpected violence of the Confederates, had thrown up strong earthworks and cut down trees before them. The General, who was going to make his enemy "ingloriously fly," had taken a strong defensive position. Attack on it would be suicidal.

In the face of such facts Jackson and Lee talked after dark came on. Jackson believed that something had gone wrong with Hooker's offensive. "By tomorrow," he said, "there will not be any of them on this side of the river." Lee did not agree. He studied a map. They had reports that despite Hooker's strength before them his right flank was "in the air." By that they meant that his line ended unprotected by any hill, stream, fortification or other natural or artificial barrier.

"How can we get at those people?"

And loyal Stonewall said: "You know best. Show me what to do, and we will try to do it."

Then Lee gave Jackson the order to take his troops around the Yankees. The plan was as dangerous as it was audacious. Only such a man as Stonewall could be entrusted to dare it. Old Jack rose from the log, saluted, and told Lee, "My troops will move at four o'clock."

In the resplendent uniform which Stuart had given him Jackson slept on the ground in the chill night. He began to catch a bad cold. His sword, which he had leaned against a tree, fell without any apparent cause and an officer who noted it feared that meant bad luck. In the dim first light of morning when Jackson was up eagerly drinking a cup of hot coffee, Lee joined him again by the campfire. Both understood the hazards they faced. If Hooker attacked before Jackson hit him either in the Wilderness or with his force back at Fredericksburg, Lee's troops might be caught in a crushing pincers. They studied a map showing a road on which Jackson might move with dispatch.

Then Lee asked calmly, "General Jackson, what do you propose to do?"

Jackson's finger followed the line of the road. "Go around here."

"What do you propose to make this movement with?"

"My whole corps," Stonewall said. His plan was not a diversionary attack so Lee could hit Hooker in front, but a decisive victory.

"What will you leave me?" Lee asked quietly. And Old Jack said two divisions, just 14,000 men to face Hooker's vast forces.

Lee indicated his great confidence casually. "Well, go on," he said.

With little delay Stonewall marched at 8 A.M. The war blaze was in his eyes. His men moved smartly, eagerly, and quietly so as not to warn the enemy. Habitually Jackson said, "Close up, press on," but the order was hardly needed. He seemed in a happy mood when he rode Little Sorrel up to the van and found himself in the company of three other former professors at V.M.I. and Colonel Tom Munford, of the Second Virginia Cavalry. He had been cadet adjutant at V.M.I. on the day Jackson arrived and the cadets made jokes from the ranks about his big feet. They talked of old times. And a little later as Jackson gave Munford an order, he called after that young officer as he prepared to gallop away, "The Institute will be heard from today."

It was to General Robert E. Rodes, old V.M.I. professor, to whom Jackson gave a historic command. The troops had made their march. The necessary roads had been found to bring the corps secretly and audaciously to its destination. Then Jackson with "a brilliant glow" in his eyes rode forward and saw through the thick underbrush the unraveled right and rear of Hooker's great army, men at ease, lines of stacked guns, fires preparing supper. It was four o'clock. The moment had come.

"Are you ready, General Rodes?"

"Yes, sir."

"Then," said Stonewall, "you can go forward."

In the quiet woods a Rebel bugler sounded a blast. Others blared loudly. The Confederates swept forward in such swift, massed attack that they drove rabbit and deer before them toward the Federal lines. And above them as they came sounded the high-pitched Rebel Yell. Hooker's right and rear melted in a rout. Men in blue died before they knew what had hit them. But even in the confusion the frightening word spread that these screaming fellows were Stonewall Jackson's men.

Only the sun disturbed the General. Though he sometimes seemed a Biblical kind of figure, he was no Joshua to make the sun stand still. And in the tangled woods only the dusk threatened his advance. Night came on and still Jackson pressed his men forward till in the headlong drive their own regiments became mixed up and intermingled. Even in the dark Jackson meant to hurl the Federal forces into the river. Careless as always of danger to himself, despite the protests of his staff, he rode forward in the moonlight along the tangled lines of fighting men.

He was seeking a road which might make it possible to pinch Hooker into a vise to be squeezed by his forces and Lee's. On the way he met his old V.M.I. student, General Jim Lane, now commanding a division of North Carolina troops. Lane's men were ready for a further attack. He asked Jackson for the order to advance.

★ 169 ☆

Stonewall slumped in his saddle. Little Sorrel ran

unreined and Jackson's head struck the limb of a tree.

"Push right ahead, Lane."

And Jackson pushed forward, too, looking for the road. Instead, he found himself close to the enemy, who were felling trees in the dark, entrenching themselves. Jackson and his staff turned back. Between the lines their horses made sounds like a detachment of cavalry. And in the dark, Jim Lane's North Carolina troops let loose a volley.

"Cease firing! Cease firing!" one of Jackson's companions shouted.

Another called, "Cease firing. You are firing into our own men."

But in the dark an officer shouted, "Who gave that order? It's a lie. Pour it into them, boys!"

Stonewall slumped in his saddle. Little Sorrel ran unreined and the wounded General's head struck the limb of a tree. Under much gunfire, those who tried to save Jackson dropped the litter on which they were carrying him. He was uncomplaining but in great pain. His left arm was amputated that night.

The Federal Army, though badly beaten, was not destroyed as Jackson hoped it might be. Next morning the Confederates under the dashing Stuart hit them harder and again. Fighting Joe Hooker, dazed in the battle, felt like fighting no more. And next morning, too, Lee, with even more emotion than his message showed, sent Jackson a note: "Could I have directed events, I should have chosen for the good of the country to be disabled in your stead. I congratulate you on the victory, which is due to your skill and energy."

"General Lee is very kind," said Jackson, "but he should have given the praise to God."

Stonewall's wounds were healing. He seemed better. He rejoiced in the reports of the battle, particularly of the fine fighting of his old Stonewall Brigade. It remained dear to him though other men led it. Its last commander was to be General James A. Walker, who as a cadet at V.M.I. had so resented Jackson's discipline that he had threatened the professor with violence. All such things were far behind.

"Some day the men of that brigade," said Old Jack to those about his bed, "will be proud to say to their children, 'I was one of the Stonewall Brigade.' The name belongs to them, not to me."

He went to sleep that night free of pain.

14

The Shade of the Trees

As Jackson continued to improve Lee sent him another message: "Give him my affectionate regards, and tell him to make haste and get well, and come back to me as soon as he can. He has lost his left arm, but I have lost my right."

Old Jack blushed at the praise of the commander whom he had said he was ready to follow blindfolded. He did not protest when he was moved farther to the rear. He was sure now that he had been spared by Providence. For recuperation he chose to go to the plantation of some friends near his old headquarters at Moss Neck. And there on May 6, 1863, four days after he was wounded, young Dr. Hunter Mc-Guire, who had served with Jackson throughout the war, felt that his famous patient was so much better that he could give himself the luxury of long needed sleep.

But Jackson woke in the morning nauseated. There were violent pains in his right side. Reluctantly the General permitted McGuire to be awakened. Only brief examination was needed by the doctor to show him that pneumonia had set in. When Anna arrived that same day, after a hard journey to her husband's bedside with their baby, she was terrified by his appearance. Jackson cheered her. "My darling, you must cheer up and not wear a long face. I love cheerfulness and brightness in a sick room." But he seemed not able to hear all she said. He whispered, "My darling, you are very much beloved."

Then he was incoherent. He issued commands to his troops. But his own long, last retreat had begun.

In the custom of those days Anna, told by the doctors that he could not live, had to tell him so. Clear in his mind then, he accepted her choking statement that he would soon be in Heaven. He was ready to go. "Yes, I prefer it, I prefer it!" Then his much-loved little daughter was brought into the room. And the child smiled happily as he caressed her. Then he sank into a haze, and when he emerged he tried again to comfort Anna. He asked her to call Dr. McGuire.

"Doctor, Anna informs me that you have told her that I am to die today; is it so?"

Yes, McGuire told him. Jackson stared for a moment at the ceiling.

"Very good, very good, it is all right."

The room was still but for the General's terrible breathing. Then his voice rose clearly in commands . . . *"Prepare for action! . . . pass the infantry to the front!"* He thundered, then quieted. He lay very still. Then at the last in a very soft voice, he said:

"Let us cross over the river, and rest under the shade of the trees."

That was Sunday, May 10, 1863. Stonewall was thirty-nine years old. The South had won a great battle, one which, some Southerners thought, would lead to the end of the war. But the Confederacy had lost Stonewall Jackson. And the war had to go on. When the corps of V.M.I. cadets marched sadly and proudly with Jackson's cortege to the grave in Lexington, where he had asked to be buried, Lee was already planning another such movement into the North as his lost lieutenant had steadily urged from the beginning of the war. And in Pennsylvania, at Gettysburg, less than two months after Jackson's death, the ragged Confederates charged through withering gunfire to their high point in valor and hope on Cemetery Ridge. The result might have been different if Jackson had been there. Lee himself, who never spoke rashly, said, "If I had had Jackson at Gettysburg, I should have won the battle, and a complete victory there would have resulted in the establishment of Southern independence."

Perhaps so. Not even the conjectures of great generals, however, are certainties. What is certain is that the two years in which Stonewall fought were the years of victories against odds in the Confederacy's struggle for its cause. Even more certain it is that

Thomas Jonathan Jackson, Stonewall, Professor Jackson, Old Jack—perhaps even Fool Tom, as young cadets called him before they fought with him—rode Little Sorrel into long remembrance. He pressed on into the most precious legends of a South which never lost the love of its heroes. He marched, too, into the heritage of a reunited nation which recalls greatness now regardless of whether it then wore gray or blue.

A young Southern poet named John Esten Cooke, who was also a cavalryman who rode with Stonewall, spoke best for Jackson's soldiers after Chancellorsville. In "The Song of the Rebel" he wrote:

> In all the days of future years
> His name and fame shall shine—
> The stubborn, iron captain
> Of our old Virginia Line!
> And men shall tell their children,
> Though all other memories fade,
> That they fought with Stonewall Jackson
> In the old "Stonewall Brigade!"

INDEX

★ 179 ☆

LANDMARK BOOKS

WORLD LANDMARK BOOKS